Resistance: Stories from World War II France

Édith Thomas and her nephews, Daniel Thomas and Jacques Thomas. Photograph by Madeleine Thomas. Used with permission of Daniel Thomas and Jacques Thomas.

ÉDITH THOMAS

Resistance: Stories from World War II France

Translated by

Michelle Chilcoat

Introduction by

Michelle Chilcoat and Lori J. Marso

Foreword by

Dorothy Kaufmann

Modern Language Association of America

New York 2022

Library of Congress Cataloging-in-Publication Data
Names: Thomas, Édith, author. | Chilcoat, Michelle, translator. | Chilcoat, Michelle, writer of introduction. | Marso, Lori Jo, writer of introduction. | Kaufmann, Dorothy, writer of foreword.
Title: Resistance: stories from World War II France / Édith Thomas ; translated by Michelle Chilcoat ; introduction by Michelle Chilcoat and Lori J. Marso ; foreword by Dorothy Kaufmann. Other titles: Contes d'Auxois. English
Description: New York : Modern Language Association of America, 2022. | Series: Texts and translations ; 10792538 ; 34 | Includes bibliographical references. | Summary: "An English translation of short stories by Édith Thomas (1909–70), first published as Contes d'Auxois. Portrays resistance by ordinary people during the Nazi occupation of Vichy France in World War II. Explores the nature of heroism, the identity of one's allies and enemies, and the ways individuals can find solidarity"— Provided by publisher.
Identifiers: LCCN 2021021187 (print) | LCCN 2021021188 (ebook) | ISBN 9781603295024 (paperback) | ISBN 9781603295031 (EPUB)
Subjects: LCSH: World War, 1939–1945—France—Fiction. | France—History—German occupation, 1940–1945—Fiction. | LCGFT: Short stories.
Classification: LCC PQ2639.H56 C613 2022 (print) | LCC PQ2639.H56 (ebook) | DDC 843/.912—dc23
LC record available at https://lccn.loc.gov/2021021187
LC ebook record available at https://lccn.loc.gov/2021021188

Texts and Translations 34

ISSN 1079-2538

Cover illustration: *Honneur au Maquis*. c. 1941. Mary Evans Picture Library / Grenville Collins Postcard Collection.

Published by The Modern Language Association of America
85 Broad Street, Suite 500, New York, New York 10004-2434
www.mla.org

Édith Thomas. *Contes d'Auxois*. Les Éditions de Minuit, 1943. Translated by permission of Daniel Thomas.

Contents

Foreword: Writing Underground

Dorothy Kaufmann

Édith Thomas played a crucial role in what the French call *la Résistance intellectuelle* (the intellectual resistance), the struggle to counter Nazi and Vichy propaganda by giving voice to forbidden discourse. She was the lone woman in the Paris network of French Resistance writers and contributed her *Contes d'Auxois*, published here as *Stories of Resistance*, as well as articles and poems, to the underground press. Michelle Chilcoat's excellent translation revives these stories for English-speaking readers, and as Chilcoat and Lori Marso emphasize in their informative introduction, *Contes d'Auxois* contains tales of "everyday acts of resistance," in which ordinary French women and men—and even a German soldier—say no to the occupying Nazi forces.

After the trauma of France's collapse and occupation by Nazi Germany, the majority of French people chose neither resistance nor active collaboration but various forms of accommodation with the Germans. Resistance was the response of a small minority. Thomas's immediate response to the occupation is a harbinger of that resistance. On 25 June 1940, the day the armistice with Germany took effect, Thomas writes in her diary: "On va nous apprendre désormais à haïr tout ce que nous avions aimé et ce que nous avions raison d'aimer. On va désormais nous apprendre que c'est la raison qui a tort et la folie et le désespoir qui sont la plus grande sagesse" ("They are going to teach us now to hate everything we loved and were right to love. They are going to teach us that reason is wrong and madness and despair are the greatest wisdom"; *Pages* 77; Kaufmann 67). She goes on to warn her compatriots of what lies ahead: "des cimetières et des camps de concentration, l'ordre moral des morts" ("cemeteries and concentration camps, the moral order of the dead"; 78; 67). A few weeks later, she asks herself: "Que peut-on *faire*?" ("What can one *do*?"; 88; 68). What she could do was serve the Resistance by writing.

Writing for the underground press, like every other kind of resistance, was dangerous; censorship laws severely restricted the information that could be released and the themes that could be developed in publications. A series of regulations pertaining to the production and distribution of undesirable publications reinforced the censorship laws. Another law stipulated that anyone who received anti-German tracts had to inform the local Kommandantur, or military headquarters. Persons who helped distribute tracts were warned that they would be among the first hostages.

In October 1940 Raymond Deiss, a cousin of Thomas's father, began printing and distributing the first underground publication of the occupation, *Pantagruel*, named after the irreverent Renaissance hero in François Rabelais's novel *Gargantua and Pantagruel*. Each issue of *Pantagruel* appeared in linotype on two double sheets that were clearly and elegantly typed. In 1941 Deiss was arrested, along with his two associates. None of them survived. Deiss was sent to prison in Cologne, Germany, and later was decapitated with an ax. The modest aim of his journal had been "le maintien de notre droit millénaire à penser par nous-mêmes" ("to preserve our thousand-year-old right to think for ourselves"; qtd. in Bellanger 34; Kaufmann 85).

In 1942 Thomas began writing for the underground publication *Les lettres françaises* (*French Letters*), which at the time consisted of a few sheets reproduced on a mimeograph. Thomas headlined her first article in large, bold calligraphic letters, "Crier la vérité!" ("Cry Out the Truth!").[1] In the article she speaks about what she has witnessed: "les étoiles sur les poitrines, l'arrachement des enfants aux mères, les hommes qu'on fusille chaque jour, la dégradation méthodique de tout un peuple" ("the yellow star, children snatched from their mothers' arms, men shot every day, the methodical degradation of an entire people"; 1; Kaufmann 88). The article was a call to writers to be faithful to their vocation, which meant crying out the truth of what they saw happening around them.

Thomas's *Contes d'Auxois* was published in 1943 by Les Éditions de Minuit (The Midnight Editions), an astonishing underground publishing house that had no equivalent anywhere in occupied Europe. The purpose of Les Éditions de Minuit was twofold: to make it possible for French writers to be published in France without having to submit to censorship, and, just as important, to project to the world an image of France that would counter the image projected by the Vichy government. Although a clandestine publishing house would seem to be an oxymoron, Pierre de Lescure and Jean Bruller, the founders of Les Éditions de Minuit, were determined to produce a series of volumes free of any concession to the enemy, books that would show real literary value and demonstrate to the world that the French spirit was still alive. In a further act of defiance, the presentation of each book was aesthetically of high quality, from the paper and the typography to the book's binding. All the difficulties of production and distribution confronted by underground tracts and newspapers were compounded in this far more ambitious enterprise; there was also the problem of finding authors willing to publish books under conditions that not only were dangerous but also required anonymity.

Yvonne Paraf, the woman who bound books for the publisher in her home, had the idea of designating Les Éditions de Minuit authors by the regions of France with which they felt a special connection. Most of the stories in *Contes d'Auxois*, taken from real events, are set in or around Sainte-Aulde, a village on the Marne River where Thomas's mother lived in the family home. Thomas may have adapted her pseudonym, Auxois, from the name of a neighboring village, Orxois.

The change in the note at the back of each volume published by Les Éditions de Minuit is revealing. In volumes published before 1943, the note reads: "Ce volume publié aux dépens d'un patriote a été achevé d'imprimer sous l'occupation nazie" ("The printing of this volume, published at the expense of a patriot, was completed under Nazi occupation"; Vercors)—and ends with the publication date.[2] In 1943, the note was revised for new publications: "un patriote" ("a patriot") was changed to "quelques gens de lettres patriotes" ("a few patriotic people of letters"), and "sous l'occupation nazie" ("under Nazi occupation") became simply "sous l'oppression" ("under oppression"; Thomas, *Contes*). Significantly, the word "Nazi" was never replaced with "allemand" ("German") because the contributors decided not to treat the terms as synonyms. The anti-Nazi German soldier Hans in Thomas's story "Lime Blossom Tea" embodies the distinction between the terms. As Thomas points out in the testimony collected in *La Résistance intellectuelle*, the literature of the Resistance was written to fight against an ideology of human degradation; it refused to characterize a racial or national difference, the French in opposition to the Germans ("Édith Thomas" 61). For Thomas, the defeat of German civilization in 1933, when Adolf Hitler came to power in Germany, was no less real than the military defeat of France in 1940.

Les Éditions de Minuit published thirty-three books between February 1942 and the liberation of Paris in August 1944; each one had the same elegant presentation and was small enough to fit into a coat pocket. Thomas took pleasure in registering the copyright of each volume at the Bibliothèque Nationale, where she worked, without the knowledge of either her comrades or the head administrator at the library, Bernard Faÿ, an enthusiastic Nazi collaborator who had been appointed to replace Julien Cain, who was Jewish.

For a long time Thomas had been determined to make contact with the Francs-Tireurs et Partisans (Partisan Irregular Riflemen), the Communist-led guerrilla group featured in "FTP," the final story in *Contes d'Auxois*, so that she could write about them for the clandestine press. Thomas's diary entry for 30 April 1944 consists only of a series of dashes to mark the date of her departure for the maquis, which she had been preparing to join for many months with the help of Resistance comrades. She made contact with the Francs-Tireurs et Partisans in the Cévennes Mountains of southern France and published the first account of her experience in *Les lettres françaises* in June 1944, a few weeks before the liberation of Paris.

Thomas's courage in the Resistance was prefigured in her personal struggle with extreme illness. In 1931, when Thomas was twenty-two years old, she was diagnosed with tuberculosis of the bone, a disease that attacked her knee, keeping her bedridden and in intense pain for three years. The ordeal left her in fragile health, with a permanent limp. From that period of distress, she developed a fierce and ongoing determination to give her life meaning. During the traumatic years of Nazi occupation, Thomas found that meaning in her choice to resist—to say no—with the force she had: the written word.

Notes

1. See Kaufmann 87 for a reproduction of page 1 of the second issue of *Les lettres françaises.*

2. Unless otherwise indicated, translations are mine.

Works Cited

Bellanger, Claude. *La presse clandestine, 1940–1944.* Armand Colin, 1962.

Kaufmann, Dorothy. *Édith Thomas: A Passion for Resistance.* Cornell UP, 2004.

Thomas, Édith. *Contes d'Auxois.* Les Éditions de Minuit, 1943.

———. "Crier la verité!" *Les lettres françaises*, no. 2, Oct. 1942, pp. 1–2.

———. "Édith Thomas nous apporte quelques précisions." *La Résistance intellectuelle*, edited by Jacques Debû-Bridel, Juillard, 1970, pp. 54–64.

———. *Pages de journal, 1939–1944.* Pages de journal, 1939–1944, *suivies de* Journal intime de monsieur Célestin Costedet, edited by Dorothy Kaufmann, Éditions Viviane Hamy, 1995, pp. 37–221.

Vercors (Jean Bruller). *Le silence de la mer.* Les Éditions de Minuit, 1942.

Introduction

Michelle Chilcoat and Lori J. Marso

Édith Thomas: Restoring Women to the History of French Resistance

Working as archivist and then as senior conservator in the Archives Nationales (National Archives) in Paris for most of her adult life, Édith Thomas was an accomplished novelist, poet, short story writer, journalist, and pioneer in the discipline of women's history. Thomas must also be counted among a number of women whose participation in the French Resistance was without question crucial to the liberation of France. But to appreciate the significance of Thomas's contribution to the cause, one must consider the developing history of women in the Resistance.

Many factors have contributed to our increased understanding of how women participated in resisting Vichy-Nazi and then Nazi rule. Factors contributing to this greater understanding have included the ever-mounting urgency in locating and hearing firsthand from the last living witnesses to those events, the 2015 opening of World War II–era archives to the public, and the rapid digitization of materials in those archives and their accessibility through the Internet (as well as, for documents not yet digitized, indications on the Internet of where they are held and how they might be consulted). The year 2015 was also notable for the commemoration of two female members of the French Resistance, Germaine Tillion and Charles de Gaulle's niece Geneviève de

Gaulle-Anthonioz, whose remains were interred in the Panthéon for their crucial efforts in the liberation.

If the roles women played in the French Resistance have taken such a long time to become a sustained subject of historical and political attention, it is in part because of a longstanding belief, including among many French women, that even if they did participate actively, it would not be womanly to say so (unless their participation entailed nursing or knitting socks for the men in the Resistance). Silent and invisible behind the man or men in her life, a good French woman, according to this belief, was self-effacing, a martyr to the cause who might not even see herself as such. War was understood to involve men, not women; the *femme guerrière* (woman soldier) was seen as no longer a woman and certainly not a man, but instead an aberration. Yet in the wake of two world wars, it was undeniable that women had had to fill the shoes of the men who went off to fight those wars and that women had demonstrated that they could indeed do anything men did when the situation demanded it.

And for a brief moment after the liberation of Paris, a few of the women who had played active parts throughout the Resistance were officially recognized for their contributions alongside their far more numerous fellow *combattants de l'ombre* (shadow combatants), as Resistance fighters were commonly called. Newsreel footage shows, for example, twenty-year-old Madeleine Riffaud sitting atop a tank and waving to the jubilant crowds that lined Paris streets to welcome their liberators in 1944.[1] Between 1940 and 1945, six women were among the 1,036 people awarded the Croix de la Libération (the Liberation Cross; World War II's most prestigious decoration).[2] Some *femmes résistantes* (Resistance women) were even appointed delegates of the Assemblée Consultative Provisoire (Provisionary Consultative Assembly), including Lucie

Aubrac,[3] Gilberte Brossolette, Marie-Hélène Lefaucheux, Marthe Simard, and Marie-Claude Vaillant-Couturier.[4] Recognizing that many women had joined the secret work of the Resistance in the country's fight for freedom and had "payé un lourd tribut à la barbarie nazie" ("paid a heavy price under Nazi barbarism"), including as "combattantes des barricades" ("fighters on the barricades"), a Parisian campaign poster encouraged women, who would be exercising their newly won right to vote for the first time in the 1945 municipal elections, to run for office so as to "continuer votre participation dans la vie nationale" ("continue to participate in the life of the nation"; qtd. in Musée 242).[5] Several women ran in 1945 for seats in the first Assembly of the Fourth Republic, but women took only five percent of the seats, and unfortunately, they took a progressively smaller proportion in the ensuing years (Quétel 232).

Since then, the *femmes résistantes* have had a harder time retaining their place in the annals of French history. Of course, the history of the Resistance has always been difficult to recover because resistance activity is by its nature clandestine and because those who participated in the Resistance did so under pseudonyms or completely anonymously. But identifying the women who participated in the making of that history is further complicated by the ambiguities of gender. Disguising herself in an exaggerated femininity to distract Vichy officials, for example, a *femme résistante* could carry out resistance activities right under their noses. On the other hand, *femmes résistantes* often played down or masked their femininity when among male resistance fighters, who likely resented the presence of women in their ranks. While both tactics facilitated the active participation of *femmes résistantes* in the Resistance, both also contributed to their invisibility, making it easier for subsequent histories of the Resistance to ignore them.

Nevertheless, as a result of the increased focus on women in commemorations of the seventieth anniversary of the liberation of France and the seventy-fifth anniversary of the Normandy landings, the nature of resistance activity more broadly has been reassessed, and deified Resistance heroes such as Charles de Gaulle and Jean Moulin have been resituated within the context of the ordinary French people who made the liberation possible. These changes have been especially useful for reconsidering the two prevailing tendencies in understanding how the French people responded to their country's humiliating 1940 defeat by Nazi Germany. The first tendency, dominant from the beginning of the liberation in 1944 to the December 1964 transferal of Moulin's ashes to the Panthéon under de Gaulle's presidency, held that a majority of the French supported the Resistance and united behind it. The second tendency, emerging on the heels of the May 1968 mass student and worker demonstrations against the reigning hierarchies of social and political power, sought to expose the extent of French collaboration during the occupation years. In *Les résistants: L'histoire de ceux qui refusèrent* (*Resistance Fighters: The History of Those Who Refused*), Robert Belot suggests (5) that this latter tendency culminated in the decision by the Archives Nationales to commemorate the seventieth anniversary of the country's liberation with its exhibition *La collaboration (1940–1945)* (*The Collaboration [1940–1945]*), the first of its kind in France.

Les résistants is an important publication in that it represents an antidote to the tendencies described above: it endeavors to situate the Resistance "dans toute sa complexité, dans toute sa diversité" ("in all its complexity and all its diversity"), namely through a focus on the men and women "qui l'ont faite" ("who made it happen") but who were at the same time often motivated by "des rivalités, des divergences de conception, des ambitions humaines, trop humaines" ("rivalries, disagreements, and human—all too human—ambition"; Belot 5). *Les résistants* also broadens and refines what it meant to resist in World War II France by approaching resistance activity in terms of three principle functions, "la propagande, le renseignement, et l'action paramilitaire" ("propaganda, intelligence, and paramilitary action"). More significantly, perhaps, the study recounts how resistance propaganda produced at the beginning of the occupation laid the groundwork for the Resistance's intelligence and paramilitary action (37). With all media (print, radio, cinema, etc.) under their strict control and censorship, Vichy and occupation forces attempted to isolate France from the rest of the world, launching a massive propaganda campaign aimed at terrorizing the French into believing that the Vichy-Nazi collaboration represented their only hope against Communists and Jews—who, according to the fascists, were the real enemies.

The Resistance, therefore, first had to fight a psychological war aimed at shifting the mentality of a civilian population that, in the absence of reliable information, was either apathetic toward, or believed it had to resign itself to, the devastating defeat by the German army, which took 1.8 million French soldiers as prisoners of war. Yet even before Adolf Hitler declared war on the country, there were men and women in France who had been deeply concerned by the rise of fascist movements throughout Europe over the previous decade of economic crisis and who had, for example, fought in the Spanish Civil War or founded and written for newspapers in order to keep the public informed of the fascist threat. Thus, in Philippe Pétain's announcement of armistice and then of collaboration between Germany and France, these French people saw nothing less than the enslavement of their country under Nazi rule. Thomas must be included among these men and women whose voices and writings contributed early on to resistance against the rising wave of fascism across Europe.

Lost in the shadows of more famous intellectual power couples such as Simone de Beauvoir and Jean-Paul Sartre, and Elsa Triolet and Louis Aragon, Thomas remains largely unfamiliar to both French and English readers. To remedy this situation, Dorothy Kaufmann's impressively documented 2004 biography, *Édith Thomas: A Passion for Resistance* (translated into French in 2007), provides the historical, political, and literary contexts, as well as the particular life circumstances, that shaped Thomas's writings. Kaufmann's thorough archival research and numerous interviews with Thomas's colleagues, friends, and family members reveal Thomas in her many dimensions. For instance, Thomas did not fear solitude but actively set herself apart in situations that she believed called for an open demonstration of her commitment to a principled life. Born to nonpracticing Catholic parents who, while politically conservative, were open-minded and tolerant, she describes becoming a Protestant at age sixteen not as an expression of rebellion or religious belief but more succinctly as "le premier acte de ma liberté" ("the first act of my freedom"; *Témoin compromis* 40) She would continue to enact this freedom, which she understood as exercising the capacity to think and act independently of others, even at the risk of incurring emotional or physical injury. In fact, commitment in and of itself was a guiding principle for Thomas throughout her life.

Fascism was on the rise across Europe when the twenty-year-old Thomas entered the École Nationale des Chartes (National School of Charters) in 1929 to pursue a degree in medieval history and archival studies. Her open hostility toward the extreme right singled her out in the conservative

Catholic milieu. Diagnosed with tuberculosis of the bone after graduating in 1931 (and having contended with intense and persistent pain in her left knee throughout her studies), Thomas spent the greater part of the following two years in isolation and confined to bed. During that time, she discovered communism and her need to write, producing manuscripts for two novels, *La mort de Marie* (*The Death of Marie*) and *L'homme criminal* (*The Criminal Man*). *La mort de Marie*, a haunting account of the main character's lonely yet ecstatic suffering and death by tuberculosis, received France's Prix de premier roman (First Novel Prize); both works were published in 1934 by Éditions Gallimard (still one of France's most prestigious presses).

Her long bout with a potentially fatal illness left Thomas emotionally and physically exhausted and permanently handicapped. Considering herself unmarriageable as an independent-minded and now disabled woman, Thomas questioned the point of her existence when she was so financially precarious that her main preoccupation involved insuring her next meal. Profound depression and suicidal thoughts, however, fueled Thomas's resolve to revolt against suffering, hers and that of others, especially after she witnessed the brutalities of French colonialism during a brief period she spent recuperating in Algeria in 1934. Upon her return to France, she sought work writing for left-wing newspapers in Paris; the newly founded anti-fascist newspaper *Vendredi* (*Friday*) published her first articles, a series on the hardships particular to women workers. Brief membership in the Association des Écrivains et Artistes Révolutionnaires (Association of Revolutionary Writers and Artists) connected her with the surrealist author Louis Aragon, who hired her as a journalist for the Communist newspaper he published, *Ce Soir* (*This Evening*). Between 1935 and 1938, Thomas contributed numerous articles on social problems in Paris, including the lamentable living conditions of aged workers and the need for health and education programs for impoverished children. Despite her limp and her fragile health, she also took on dangerous assignments, in Spain reporting for the Republican side of the Spanish Civil War, and in Austria carrying out secret interviews on the rise of Nazism in the year preceding the Anschluss.

Just after Aragon fired her from *Ce Soir* in mid-1938 because of differences of opinion related to his hardline communism, Thomas contracted tuberculosis again, of the lungs this time, and had to leave Paris for another long, painful treatment. In September 1941, Thomas returned to an occupied Paris, fully committed to fighting Hitler and Nazism. Despite misgivings stemming in part from her experiences with Aragon, she joined the Communist Party in 1942, as it offered the best way to hook up with the Resistance, which she had become determined to do the moment she learned of its activity. That same year, after the Gestapo arrested and executed Jacques Decour, the original editor of the clandestine newspaper *Les lettres françaises* (*French Letters*), before he could get the first issue out, Thomas signed on as coeditor (anonymously of course). She composed hard-hitting yet compassionate articles for the paper such as "Crier la vérité!" ("Cry Out the Truth!"), in which she excoriates French literati who feel obliged as artists to "s'isoler dans [leur] tour d'ivoire" ("isolate in their ivory tower"), refusing to break their silence even as the cattle car of a French train passes them by, filled with children whose cries for "Maman" ("Mama") go unanswered. As Kaufmann mentions in her foreword to this volume, Thomas also contributed reports on the activity of Resistance fighters in several maquis groups throughout France after managing to visit them in spring 1944. The sole woman on the Comité National des Écrivains (National Committee of Writers), which also included Sartre and Albert Camus, among others, Thomas opened her apartment at 15 rue Pierre Nicole (in the fifth arrondissement) to meetings of the intellectual resistance from February 1943 until the liberation. A commemorative plaque, installed in March 2013 at that address, now reminds passersby that Thomas risked her life to host such meetings, since hosting them was a crime punishable by execution under Nazi law, and in August 2019—seventy-five years after the liberation of Paris—the Place Édith Thomas was established at the Porte d'Orléans (fig. 1).[6]

Thomas also took part, along with Pierre de Lescure, Jean Bruller (better known by his pen name, Vercors), and Yvonne Paraf, in establishing Les Éditions de Minuit (The Midnight Editions) and helped distribute its publications at the risk of arrest, deportation, and execution.[7] In 1943, after the 1942 publication of Vercor's international bestseller *Le silence de la mer* (*The Silence of the Sea*), the press published Thomas's pseudonymous *Contes d'Auxois*, republished in this volume as

Figure 1. Place Édith Thomas. Photograph by Michelle Chilcoat.

Stories of Resistance, a collection of seven short stories that narrate extraordinary acts of resistance by ordinary people whom Thomas had personal knowledge of. Upon word of the liberation of France's capital in August 1944, Thomas dared to leave her Paris apartment, as bullets continued to fly, in order to take notes on the event directly from the barricades; 1945 saw the publication of her book *La libération de Paris* (*The Liberation of Paris*), which is based on her eyewitness account. She also completed a biography of Joan of Arc, which she undertook in order to redeem the woman warrior from the far right's exploitative depiction of her. At the Communist Party's behest Thomas also agreed to edit *Femmes françaises*, a journal for the Union des Femmes Françaises (French Women's Union), from which she would resign immediately after the war because she was unable to cope with the editorial board's limiting of women's issues to concerns for family and household.

Between 1947 and 1949, Thomas experienced two great heartbreaks. The first was the ending of a brief but intense love affair with the Éditions Gallimard editor Dominique Aury (with whom Thomas nevertheless remained in close contact for the rest of her life). Aury was the woman who anonymously authored *Histoire d'O* (*The Story of O*), a highly controversial novel featuring female masochistic erotica and a character partly inspired by Thomas. The second heartbreak came with Thomas's decision—provoked by the Tito affair—to resign from the Communist Party.[8] Thomas harbored no illusions regarding the social death she would experience the moment she quit the party in 1949, and contrary to most of those who left the party, Thomas did so openly, in a letter published on 15 December in the leftist newspaper *Combat*.

Resisting the suicidal thoughts that arose within her once again, Thomas wrote several impressively documented historical biographies of powerful nineteenth-century women, including George Sand, Pauline Roland, and Louise Michel, distinguishing herself as a pioneer in the discipline of women's history. In almost all her writing, she turned to fictional characters or real people with whom she identified but who were uniquely shaped by their circumstances and particular moment in history. Thomas's own circumstances and moment aligned perhaps most closely with the main character of her last novel, published shortly before she died suddenly from viral hepatitis in 1970. In *Le jeu d'échecs* (*The Chess Game*), despite the potentially pessimistic title (which translates literally as *The Game of Failures*), the main character, Aude, who is resolutely single and has just given birth to a little girl, finally sees that the reason for existence is "l'aventure d'amener au monde cette possibilité d'être humain" ("the adventure of bringing into the world the possibility of being human"; 265). This challenge was especially great for women, who struggled to find their place in a world created by and for men.

Thomas's unique approach to feminism runs through her publications—which, beyond seven novels, two short story collections, and six historical biographies, include hundreds of articles and reviews written for newspapers, journals, and magazines, academic as well as popular—although Thomas, much like her contemporary Simone de Beauvoir, considered the term *feminism* an outdated reference to the political and social demands of "nos grands-mères" ("our grandmothers"; *Témoin compromis* 118). Thomas referred instead to "l'humanisme féminin" ("feminine humanism"), a concept that was already being formed in her first publication, *La mort de Marie*, and that crystallized in *Le jeu d'échecs* when Aude refers to "la solidarité des femmes entre elles, dans un univers qu'elles n'ont pas fait" ("solidarity among women, in a world they did not make"; *Jeu* 261); earlier Aude observes that "[s]ans doute est-il plus facile d'être un homme qu'une femme, car il nous faut tout inventer" ("it is without a doubt easier to be a man than it is to be a woman, because we have to invent everything for ourselves"; 255). But Aude, whose life trajectory mimics Thomas's very closely, is neither bitter nor despairing here. The competitive disadvantage that has been women's lot throughout history has only rendered the so-called weaker sex that much more remarkable. Furthermore, each generation of women is deeply indebted to the one that came before for the particular improvements it currently enjoys. It is in this vein that Aude remarks: "Il y a seulement cinquante ans, je n'aurais pu être celle que j'étais aujourd'hui : si consceinte, si volontaire, si responsable" ("Only fifty years ago, I would not have been able to be who I am today: so aware, so determined, so responsible"; 255–56).

But it is not just as an expression of gratitude that Thomas trained her historian's eye on the strong women whose actions ensured better conditions for her generation; Thomas also saw the historian's task as being to take account of what has already been done so that other people—women especially—can focus instead on realizing the "possibilité d'être humain" ("possibility of being human"; *Jeu* 265). But the condition of being human cannot be achieved as long as there is war, which reduces people to the status of nonhuman animals who must struggle to meet their most basic needs, an idea clearly expressed in the first of Thomas's seven stories in *Contes d'Auxois*.

Everyday Acts of Resistance: Thomas's *Contes d'Auxois*

Contes d'Auxois introduces readers to a host of ordinary characters living through the extraordinary times of France under Nazi occupation. Each story, "transcrit du réel" ("taken from real events"), as indicated on the title page of the 1943 Les

Éditions de Minuit edition, explores the varying ways in which the characters respond to the pathological exigencies of Vichy collaborationist rule and to relentless Nazi propaganda. Confronted with their own suffering—as well as the knowledge that declared enemies of the state, including children, were being arrested, held under horrific conditions, tortured, and murdered—these characters act, in their everyday lives, in ways that challenge notions of what is heroic and what is simply human. In these stories, Thomas writes of the ordinary people, things, and situations that history tends to overlook. Readers are likely to see themselves in the lives and daily dilemmas of these characters, who, despite being unremarkable in many respects, recognize the possibility of human solidarity precisely because of the drastically reduced opportunities they have for expressing that solidarity.

Among the major preoccupations of many French intellectuals during and after the war years were the ethical and political quandaries that arose from living under the occupation. Not surprisingly, many of these intellectuals focused on determining which kinds of actions and behaviors constituted resistance to or cooperation with Nazi authorities, and what their ethical justifications could be. For example, Beauvoir, a contemporary of Thomas, wrote her famous wartime novel *Le sang des autres* (*The Blood of Others*) to address explicitly whether violence can be ethically justified when employed in the name of furthering freedom. Interestingly, Thomas and Beauvoir never met, even though Beauvoir was Sartre's partner and Thomas was a comrade of Sartre's on the Comité National des Écrivains; while both women were prolific writers on the French political left who lived through and wrote about World War II, the occupation, the trials of collaborators, debates over the meaning of Joseph Stalin's crimes, and the Algerian War, only Beauvoir achieved great literary fame, both in her time and to this day.

To appreciate the political, literary, historical, and ethical weight of Thomas's wartime writings, particularly her short stories in *Contes d'Auxois*, one may draw a comparison to Beauvoir's account of the occupation and the Resistance in *Le sang des autres*. One of the central themes in this novel is that individuals are never absolutely free, since they exist in a web of relationships in which every human choice has an impact, often unpredictable, on others both known and unknown. Beauvoir's fictional account of the occupation illustrates what happens when people engage in bad faith despite or even because of this central fact of existence. Hélène, one of the novel's main characters, lies in bed dying from an injury sustained when she attempted to carry out a violent attack on occupying German soldiers. By her bedside is Jean, a Resistance leader who reflects in anguish on his role in Hélène's impending death. His reflections are complicated by his sense of responsibility for both her individual happiness and the greater cause of French freedom. The novel is constructed mainly as a series of flashbacks, which consist of dialogues between various characters and interior monologues that ponder the potentially adverse effects of human choices.

By comparison, Thomas's stories bear witness to characters who respond to a wide variety of situations, from a woman who mutters her disgust as a German soldier passes by while she waits in the bitter cold for food supplies that will most likely run out before she gets through the line; to two young men who, despite the horrid conditions of the German work camp they have escaped, keep their promise to tell the French that not all Germans side with the Nazis and who also wonder if life after their adventure can still hold meaning for them; to a middle-aged woman who makes a cup of tea for an occupying soldier who has come down with a cold, because at that moment she sees him as some mother's son rather than as an enemy; and to six men who come together for very different reasons, risking their lives as they carry out an act of sabotage against German soldiers.

Beauvoir's use of a limited set of highly dramatic characters in extreme situations thus stands in stark contrast to Thomas's focus on ordinary people and everyday acts of resistance. For Beauvoir, fiction provides the opportunity for creating the exemplary situation necessary to illustrate the most important ethical question of life under the occupation, which is the choice to act or not act when one is aware that every choice means another human will be affected, very likely in negative ways. Beauvoir's exclusive focus on great acts of resistance that are defined above all by political subversion and violence obscures many other ethical issues that arise in the day-to-day lives of ordinary citizens, issues that are deftly portrayed by Thomas. Offering a slice of life from this time period in France, Thomas's stories in *Contes d'Auxois* play out the real choices made by people to counter the more mundane forms of brute authority that appeared under the occupation, and the stories underscore the inevitability of human responsibility toward both intimates and strangers.

Still another important difference between Thomas's and Beauvoir's World War II writing has to do with each author's level of personal engagement. Quite simply, Beauvoir did not engage in the efforts of the Resistance, whereas Thomas did. While Beauvoir sat at her table in a Paris café writing *Le sang des autres*, which she did not publish until after the war, Thomas actively wrote, published, and hosted meetings throughout the war. Thus Thomas's writing communicates a more immediate sense of how ordinary people make choices under oppressive rule. Whereas Beauvoir's ethics is most aptly understood as philosophical and abstract, Thomas's is better described as situational and concrete.

Unlike the writings of Beauvoir or Sartre from that time, in which formal existential questions play a central role, Thomas's seven stories are less distinctly linked to one particular school of philosophical thought. They instead constitute everyday ethics, an ethics that applies not only when times are extraordinary but also when they are not. These stories inspire readers to ask themselves questions like the following: How can small acts of resistance against the illegitimate imposition of authority increase feelings of solidarity among human beings? What might those identified as enemy occupiers share in the struggle against human degradation? And where and how do individuals find solidarity in a world in which the growing potential for human connectivity can also isolate and overwhelm? This two-volume edition of *Contes d'Auxois*, which presents the original French and the first English translation of the work in its entirety, will provide readers of both languages a rich opportunity to discover Thomas's important and original representations of the more ordinary truths of resistance and collaboration, as well as of the vast gray area between them.

Notes

1. This footage appears in the 2015 documentary *Résistantes*, in which Madeleine Riffaud, Cécile Rol-Tanguy, and Marie-José Chombart de Lauwe recount their experiences in the Resistance. In their nineties when they were interviewed, all three were about twenty when they joined the Resistance. Riffaud, a member of the Francs-Tireurs et Partisans (Partisan Irregular Riflemen), is among the few acknowledged French *femmes résistantes* (Resistance women) who took up arms. She was captured, tortured, and sentenced to death by the Gestapo for gun-

ning down a German soldier in Paris, by the Seine, in broad daylight. Miraculously, she was freed from prison in time to join friends fighting to liberate Paris; they took eighty German prisoners.

2. The militant feminist and anti-fascist Berty Albrecht was one of the six women awarded this honor. Albrecht and her partner Henri Frenay founded the Combat resistance network for moving Resistance fighters and escaped prisoners across the demarcation line between occupied France and the free zone. They also founded several underground newspapers, including the well-known *Combat*. Arrested and tortured by the Gestapo in 1943, Albrecht chose to hang herself rather than risk naming any members of the network. In 1947 Thomas published her *Berthie Albrecht, Pierre Arrighi, Général Brosset, D. Corticchiato, Jean Prévost: Cinq parmi d'autres (Berty Albrecht, Pierre Arrighi, General Brosset, D. Corticchiato, Jean Prévost: Five among Others)*, a preview of her pioneering work in forging the field of women's history.

3. In 1940, Lucie Aubrac and her husband Raymond Aubrac formed a small Resistance group that carried out railway sabotage, distributed tracts about the Resistance, and helped fellow *résistants* escape arrest. Aubrac is perhaps best known for successfully orchestrating her husband's escape from prison.

4. Soon after the French government banned Communism and its presses in 1939, Vaillant-Couturier participated in resistance activity, overseeing the clandestine production of Communist Party publications including *L'humanité*. She also coordinated communications among intellectual and armed Resistance groups. Arrested in February 1942, she was deported to Auschwitz-Birkenau in January 1943, in a group of two hundred and thirty *femmes résistantes* that included Danielle Casanova. Casanova joined the Communist Youth League while studying to become a dental surgeon. An ardent anti-fascist activist, Casanova contributed to clandestine presses, founded clandestine women's resistance journals, and organized demonstrations against Vichy and Nazi rule. Arrested in 1942, Casanova continued her political organizing while in Auschwitz until her death from typhus in May 1943. Thomas honored these women in her poem "Pour celles du camp d'Auschwitz" ("For Those Women in Auschwitz"), anonymously published in the December 1943 issue of *Les lettres françaises*.

5. Unless otherwise indicated, translations are by Michelle Chilcoat.

6. The plaque and the honorific street name are the results of the efforts of Thomas's nephew Daniel Thomas.

7. For more on Thomas's work for Les Éditions de Minuit, see Kaufmann's foreword in this volume.

8. When the Yugoslav dictator Josip Tito broke ties with the Soviet Union, the French Communist Party began a six-year campaign against Tito and Yugoslavia for resisting subjugation by Stalin.

Works Cited

Beauvoir, Simone de. *Le sang des autres*. Éditions Gallimard, 1945.

Belot, Robert. *Les résistants: L'histoire de ceux qui refusèrent*. Larousse, 2015.

Kaufmann, Dorothy. *Édith Thomas: A Passion for Resistance*. Cornell UP, 2004.

Musée de la Résistance Nationale. *Les résistants, 1940–1945: Récits, témoignages et documents inédits du Musée de la Résistance Nationale*. Éditions Belin, 2015.

Quétel, Claude. *Femmes dans la guerre, 1939–1945*. Larousse, 2007.

Résistantes. Directed by Pierre Hurel, featuring Madeleine Riffaud et al., Arte, 2015.

Thomas, Édith. *Contes d'Auxois*. Les Éditions de Minuit, 1943.

———. "Crier la vérité!" *Les lettres françaises*, no. 2, Oct. 1942, pp. 1–2.

———. "L'humanisme féminin." 1949. Papiers Édith Thomas, 318AP3, Archives Nationales, Paris.

———. *Le jeu d'échecs*. Grasset, 1970.

———. "Pour celles du camp d'Auschwitz." *Les lettres françaises*, no. 12, Dec. 1943, p. 3.

———. *Le témoin compromis*. Éditions Viviane Hamy, 1995.

Bibliography of Works by Édith Thomas

Novels

Le champ libre. Éditions Gallimard, 1945.

Étude de femmes. Éditions Colbert, 1945.

L'homme criminel. Éditions Gallimard, 1934.

Le jeu d'échecs. 1970. 2nd ed., Éditions Viviane Hamy, 2018.

La mort de Marie. Éditions Gallimard, 1934.

Le refus. Éditions Sociales Internationales, 1936.

Sept–sorts. Éditions Gallimard, 1935.

Short Story Collections

Contes d'Auxois. Les Éditions de Minuit, 1943.

Ève et les autres. 1952. Mercure de France, 1970.

Essay Collections, Biographies, and Historical Studies

Berthie Albrecht, Pierre Arrighi, Général Brosset, D. Corticchiato, Jean Prévost: Cinq parmi d'autres. Les Éditions de Minuit, 1947.

Les femmes de 1848. PU de France, 1948.

George Sand. Éditions Universitaires, 1960.

Jeanne d'Arc. 1947. 2nd ed., Éditions Gallimard, 1952.

La libération de Paris. Photographs by Robert Doisneau, et al., Éditions Mellottée, 1945.

Louise Michel ou la Velléda de l'anarchie. Éditions Gallimard, 1971.

Pauline Roland: Socialisme et féminisme au XIXe siècle. Librarie Marcel Rivière, 1956.

Les "pétroleuses." Éditions Gallimard, 1963.

Rossel, 1844–1871. Éditions Gallimard, 1967.

Other Works

Pages de journal, 1939–1944, *suivies de* Journal intime de monsieur Célestin Costedet. Edited by Dorothy Kaufmann, Éditions Viviane Hamy, 1995.

Le témoin compromis. 1952. Edited by Dorothy Kaufmann, Éditions Viviane Hamy, 1995.

English Translations

Eve and the Others. Translated by Estelle Eirinberg, Continental Editions, 1976.

"F.T.P." Translated by Alistair Hamilton. *Defeat and Beyond: An Anthology of French Wartime Writing, 1940–1945,* edited by Germaine Brée and George Bernauer, Pantheon Books, 1970.

Louise Michel. Translated by Penelope Williams, Black Rose Books, 1980.

"The Professor and the Mussels." Translated by Maria Jolas. *Bedside Book of Famous French Stories*, edited by Belle Becker and Robert Linscott, Random House, 1945.

The Women Incendiaries. Translated by James Atkinson and Starr Atkinson, paperback ed., Haymarket Books, 2007.

Selected Criticism and Commentary on Édith Thomas

Baty-Delande, Hélène. "Militantes: Quelles représentations de l'engagement au féminin? Sur *La femme vierge* de Madeleine Pelletier, *Délivrance* de Louise Weiss et *Le refus* d'Édith Thomas." *Journalisme et littérature de la gauche des années 1930*, edited by Anne Mathieu and François Ouellet, PU de Rennes, 2014, pp. 191–202.

Chilcoat, Michelle. "Édith Thomas (1909–1970)." *Fifty-One Key Feminist Thinkers*, edited by Lori J. Marso, Routledge, 2016, pp. 222–27.

Kaufmann, Dorothy. *Édith Thomas: A Passion for Resistance.* Cornell UP, 2004.

———. *Édith Thomas: Passionnément résistante.* Translated by Danielle Wargny, Éditions Autrement, 2007.

———. "L'humanisme féminin." *Intellectuelles: Du genre en histoire des intellectuels*, edited by Nicole Racine and Michel Trebitsch, Éditions Complexe, 2004, pp. 177–89.

———. "The Story of Two Women: Dominique Aury and Édith Thomas." *Signs*, vol. 23, no. 4, Summer 1998, pp. 883–905.

———. "Uncovering a Woman's Life: Édith Thomas (Novelist, Historian, *Résistante*)." *The French Review*, vol. 67, no. 1, Oct. 1993, pp. 61–72.

Kershaw, Angela. "Autodidacticism and Criminality in Jean-Paul Sartre's *La nausée* and Édith Thomas's *L'homme criminel*." *The Modern Language Review*, vol. 96, no. 3, July 2001, pp. 679–92.

O'Flaherty, Angela. "La Résistance Féminine: An Analysis of the Representation of Women in Selected Wartime Texts by Édith Thomas and Elsa Triolet." *French and Francophone Women Facing War / Les femmes face à la guerre*, edited by Alison S. Fell, Peter Lang, 2009, pp. 41–57.

Rochester, Myrna Bell, and Mary Lawrence Test. "Words as Hammers, Words as Bullets: Committed Fiction and French Women Writers of the Occupation Years." *Dalhousie French Studies*, vol. 54, Spring 2001, pp. 90–102.

Note on the Translation

In *Defeat and Beyond: An Anthology of French Wartime Writing, 1940–1945*, the editors Germaine Brée and George Bernauer present in English translation works written by French intellectuals during World War II that articulate a range of political and ideological positions. Édith Thomas's "FTP" appears as the last work in the anthology, one of the rare instances in which Thomas's fiction was translated into English. The editors explain that the texts included in *Defeat and Beyond* represent the "complex moods and patterns of feeling, uncertainty, [and] bafflement that underlay the simplistic either-or dialogues of traitor and patriot" (Brée and Bernauer 3). The collection belies myths erected after the war that made it seem as if everyone in France had resisted Nazi authority, aside from a few infamous collaborators. In fact, many French people—including intellectuals—were far from united in opposition to Vichy rule or even to the occupation. Well before her *Contes d'Auxois* appeared in 1943, however, Thomas had already firmly voiced her opposition in editorials, articles, and even poems urging resistance.

Stories of Resistance, my English translation of *Contes d'Auxois*, is based on the high-quality French edition originally published by Les Éditions de Minuit. Because the text was written in 1943, its language requires little updating. Thomas's clean, crisp prose further facilitated the translation process. One of the challenges of translating the work lay in the need to have a thorough understanding of its historical context, as well as of the more mundane features of daily life in France during the war. In this regard, I was fortunate to have worked with Daniel Thomas, Édith Thomas's nephew (who, along with his brother, Jacques, is executor of Thomas's literary estate), and Dorothy Kaufmann, whose painstaking research for *Édith Thomas: A Passion for Resistance*, her internationally acclaimed biography of Thomas, brought her into direct contact with a number of Thomas's closest friends and colleagues. In July 2012, Daniel and Dorothy graciously agreed to meet with me in Paris, where we sat together for hours, going through every line of the original text alongside my first complete draft of the translation. Besides answering every question I had about certain references that even the most thorough historical research could not quite elucidate, they also corrected errors I had made that were based on my interpretations of some of those references. The informative notes throughout *Stories of Resistance* are in large part the result of our discussion that day and the many e-mail exchanges and telephone conversations that continued well into 2019.

In terms of Édith Thomas's writing style, I was especially conscientious about retaining the simple yet rhythmic, sometimes poetic feel of her prose. Thomas tends to alternate frequently between past- and present-tense narration in some of the stories (most notably in "The Escapees" and "FTP"), but Anglophone readers of earlier drafts of the translation either found the tense shifts confusing or attributed them to an error on my part. For this reason, I sometimes opted to unify the tense of the narration in my translations, to the extent that I could while remaining true to the author's intentions.

Two of the seven stories in *Contes d'Auxois* have been previously published in English: "The Professor and the Mussels," Maria Jolas's 1945 translation of "Les moules et le professeur," and Alistair Hamilton's 1970 English version of "F.T.P." While both translators are well-known for their translations of the works of famous French writers, such as Nathalie Sarraute and Gaston Bachelard (by Jolas) and Georges Simenon and Georges Bataille (by Hamilton), some of the English in their translations of Thomas's stories feels dated in a way that the original French does not.

Although each story in the collection can be read separately, by going through the stories in sequence, readers can appreciate a tension that crescendos throughout the sequence as characters become inspired to resist in ever bolder ways. A key to understanding this development across the collection is Thomas's use of *The Song of Roland* in the first and final stories. In "The Mussels and the Professor," the professor compares *The Song of Roland* to a new heroic tradition that emerges in the stories shared among people waiting in the food lines outside the markets. In "FTP" a character hides a slip of paper between the pages of a school library's copy of *The Song of Roland*, and the epic poem serves as the means by which vital information gets passed on to fellow Resistance fighters, who use the information to sabotage a section of railroad track just before a train full of German soldiers is scheduled to pass by.

Work Cited

Brée, Germaine, and George Bernauer, editors. *Defeat and Beyond: An Anthology of French Wartime Writing, 1940–1945*. Pantheon, 1970.

Stories of Resistance

The Mussels and the Professor

"Sorry to disturb you, my dear," said Madame Poncelet as she opened the door to his study.

The aged professor set his pen down on a blotter and raised his head. Beyond the *Aeneid*, through a fog, her face appeared. Then the fog lifted. Jolted back to the present, the old man saw his wife, wrapped up in a flannel robe and an old black overcoat with the collar turned up around her ears. And he saw his wife's sweet face, worn yet still radiant with the secret smile she had had when she was twenty-five, back when he had married her. His life had come to depend on that secret smile ever since.

"Yes, dear, what is it?" he asked.

"You must go to the tripe shop to see if our number has come up," she said.[1] "And maybe you could stop at the fish market on the way back."

1. Madame Poncelet's comment refers to the Vichy-imposed rationing system of 1940 that issued *cartes de ravitaillement* (provisions cards) authorizing the holder to purchase indicated items (food, coal, gas, clothing, etc.) at specified times and in quantities that depended mainly on the individual's age, gender, and profession. The system drastically reduced the daily food intake of much of the French population, from at best 1,700 calories at the beginning of the occupation to 1,200 or less by the end.

"I should probably go to the fish market first," said Monsieur Poncelet.

"Whatever you prefer, my love," she said, going back into the kitchen.

He slipped on his fur-lined coat with its well-worn collar and pulled a beret down on his head. He would not have to hold on to this one, even if the wind kicked up. It was better for waiting in line. Then, after glancing over his desk with a mixture of melancholy, regret, and perhaps a little irony, he went to the kitchen to get the canvas shopping bag that had a piece of cord where the handle used to be.

"You're not going to clean the kitchen in this cold, are you?" he asked.

"Well, we can't live with this filth all winter long. Anyway, it's a little milder today."

For warmth, they only lit the fire in his study because he had to try to carry on with his important work—the most important work of his life—*The Origins of the* Aeneid. He just had to carry on, despite everything. So they had moved a sofa into his study, and that is where they slept, worked, ate, and cooked on a little hot plate.

Stirring a pot, she would say: "I'm sorry about the noise."

To which he would respond: "You know very well you're never a bother to me. Living like this has only brought us closer."

But this was not the way he had imagined either one of them spending their twilight years. No indeed, not like this.

For she was old, and he worried about the heart problems she suffered periodically, but he could not get any help for her, not even a house cleaner, because the Germans could pay much more than a retired professor could. And he and his wife could not get away to Cannes or Nice during the grayest months of the year, as he had promised they would "once he retired," because that meant crossing the demarcation line that had cut France in two;[2] on the other side things were even more expensive than in Paris because of all those rich people who had gone to live there for the duration of the war. But in Paris, at least, people felt like they were resisting. They were resisting. And so as he made his way to the fish market, the wind lashing his face (what on earth had made Annette say the weather was milder today?), the old man could almost imagine himself engaged in an act of resistance, one small but necessary link in the tenacious chain of human history.

2. Established by the armistice of June 1940 after France fell to the Germans, a 1,200-kilometer *ligne de démarcation* (demarcation line) divided Nazi-occupied France in the north and west from the so-called free zone in the southeast, which the Vichy government administered under the leadership of the *maréchal* (marshal) Philippe Pétain. By March 1943, all of France was under Nazi occupation.

There was already a line along the sidewalk, a long line of women wearing mittens and headscarves knotted beneath their chins. They were pressed up against the closed grating of the fish market, like ants on the carcass of an earthworm, ants out scrambling for food after a boot has kicked over their anthill. And did we amount to much more than that? Not a very original comparison, Monsieur Poncelet readily admitted, but who could come up with anything better in wind and cold like this? The point is, if we are constantly worried about keeping warm and finding food, what distinguishes us from animals? Human life begins beyond that. He thought for a moment about how his work *The Origins of the* Aeneid represented both the goal of his life and its justification, and he shrugged his shoulders.

All around him, he saw faces blue with cold. He recognized some from running into them on a daily basis as they waited anxiously outside the shops. He knew that one young woman had a husband who was a prisoner and that she was waiting for him to come home. But the days had become months and then years of anxious waiting on the muddy sidewalks.[3] He knew the old peasant woman with tightly pursed lips had come from somewhere deep

3. Over 2.5 million French people spent time in German captivity during the war, either as forced laborers or prisoners of war. Most of the latter (around 1.5 million in total), who were taken in 1940, were not returned to France until 1945.

in the Pyrenees "to do the lines" for her daughter who was working in a factory: "When you have two children to feed, Monsieur, and a husband who doesn't even earn enough to support himself . . ."

Spectacular news circulated by word of mouth, endlessly repeated and expanded on. For the professor, it was an opportunity to see how a people's epic history first emerges, takes shape, and then spreads.[4] This direct experience of the oral tradition made him think of Homer or *The Song of Roland*, and he smiled despite the cold.

When the fish market finally opened, the professor found himself progressing through the line by about one step every five minutes: how strange this life was.

From time to time, boot steps resounded on the sidewalk. As a soldier in a field-gray uniform was passing by,

4. I translate "la geste de tout un peuple" as "a people's epic history." Not to be confused with *le geste* (meaning "gesture" or "movement"), *la geste* refers to an ensemble of medieval epic poems that were recited before both elite and popular (i.e., illiterate) audiences and that recount, among other things, acts of wartime heroism meant to solidify a people's sense of themselves as a community or nation. *The Song of Roland* dates back to the eleventh or twelfth century and recounts a battle of Charlemagne's from the eighth century. *La geste* harks further back to classical epic poetry, such as that of Homer, as both are believed to have their origins in the oral tradition and may be either the works of individual authors or the collective and anonymous productions of a people. While these works have footing in history, how they are told and embellished is what determines their popularity and continued transmission.

one woman said behind his back: "So many of the bastards. They're like lice. When are we going to be rid of them?"

The others nodded in agreement.

At that time, French-language German newspapers were promoting collaboration between France and Germany. But the people were not fooled by this. They immediately understood what was meant by "collaboration"—long before their bourgeois counterparts did, Monsieur Poncelet noted—and it was nothing short of the enslavement of an entire continent, the most absolute subjection witnessed in centuries. Hearing the boot steps fade in the distance, Monsieur Poncelet thought about how true collaboration would not come until men had become human again. And it would not be the rulers who made that happen, but the people, just as soon as they had had enough suffering.

He could see himself in front of his students again, as he corralled them through his grand lecture on the relentless march of history.[5] Then, feeling a bit ridiculous, he smiled and took another step forward.

---

5. In the French, the professor sees himself mounted upon "le grand percheron tranquille de l'histoire," a metaphor not readily translatable into English. A Percheron is a French breed of horse highly valued for its power, endurance, intelligence, and even temperament. Both heavy and quick, it is ideal for driving and hauling as well as for riding. From the Middle Ages through World War II, the Percheron featured in war, agriculture,

Now he could see inside the shop. There were a number of large baskets, all filled with mussels.

"There will be enough for everyone," said a woman standing next to him.

"As long as no priority cases show up," added the old peasant woman in a sour tone, having loosened her tightly pursed lips just long enough to say her piece. "As long no priority cases show up.[6] How's a mother supposed to have three children if she has to watch the first two starve to death before the third one comes along?"[7]

The professor was always amazed by the common sense these women had and by their courage, their minimal complaining—a kind of unselfconscious stoicism. Deep down, human beings were actually a lot better than he thought they were when he kept to his office with his nose in a book. What might these people have become

---

transportation, and construction, after which it was replaced by technologies of the modernization it played an elemental role in bringing about.

6. Those who stood in line had to deal not only with the interminable waits and the increasing likelihood that they would go home empty-handed, while a black market catered to the French elite, Vichy operatives, and German occupiers, but also with the fact that priority cards allowed pregnant and nursing women to be served first and to buy in greater quantities, which generated animosity among the shoppers, who were mainly women. While rioting did sometimes break out, as time wore on the lines increasingly provided opportunities for demonstrations—organized largely by women—against the Vichy and Nazi regimes.

7. The peasant woman's remark alludes to Pétain's relentless probirth campaign promising material rewards to families with three or more children.

under more favorable circumstances? Who knows? Would we ever know?

Another step forward. There were not many mussels left in the baskets.

"There won't be enough for everyone," the woman standing next to him now remarked.

Humankind, what a tremendous adventure! mused the professor, even with the rush of wind biting into his nose and ears, and the absurdity of waiting hours for a pound of mussels he never even liked in the first place, and the knowledge that all this time his *Origins of the* Aeneid had not advanced by a single sentence.

"It's no use waiting any longer," said the woman standing next to him: "There won't be any left for us."

True enough, the last basket was practically empty. But Monsieur Poncelet continued to wait in line anyway, as a matter of intellectual principle, out of his need for proof and verification. So the professor did not leave until he watched the last mussel disappear into someone else's shopping basket.

He still had to stop by the tripe shop. There was no waiting there, though, because his number had not come up. Getting provisions was like playing a lottery no one ever won. Slowly, he made his way back home, the old, empty shopping bag dangling from his arm.

"So, my dear, did you bring us anything?"

"No," he answered apologetically.

He should have left a little earlier, torn himself away from the *Aeneid* on his own initiative, not waited for his wife to have to ask.

"You're freezing," she said, taking hold of his hand, "I'll make some herbal tea to warm you up."

He sat back down at his desk. He could hear his wife moving about the little portable stove. He could feel her presence.

"Have a cube of sugar," she said.

He knew she was depriving herself for him. He watched her secret smile and could feel its tenderness.

Yes, life was a remarkable adventure.

The Relief

In the newspapers they read: "Workers, depart for Germany. If you have not had to experience prison camp captivity for yourself, it is your duty to go and relieve those who have spent months behind the barbed wire, anxiously awaiting their release . . ."[1]

1. "La relève," the story's French title, is the euphemism used by the Vichy media campaign in early 1942 to pressure French workers to volunteer to go to Germany to replace German workers who had been mobilized and sent to the Russian front. Posters and front-page headlines publicized that for every three French workers (men or women) who went to work in Germany, one French prisoner of war would be returned to France. By September 1942, when it was clear the campaign had failed, the Vichy government legislated the *relève forcée* (forced relief), which designated male workers aged eighteen to fifty and female workers aged twenty-one to thirty-five as "volunteers." In February 1943, the Vichy government enforced the infamous *service du travail obligatoire* (compulsory work service; STO), applicable to all men born between 1 January 1920 and 31 December 1922. (Thomas's story, which doesn't mention the STO, was probably written before the policy was implemented.) Huge numbers of young French men headed for the maquis as a way of evading the STO. *Maquis* is a French word for terrain that is difficult to access (i.e., mountainous or heavily wooded), and it became synonymous with the Resistance because Resistance fighters—often called *maquisards*—hid in such places, where they strategized their attacks on the Nazis and on Nazi sympathizers and planned, above all, for the liberation of France.

On the clandestine radio they heard a voice, as mysterious as it was intent, chanting: "Do-not-go-to-Ger-ma-ny. Do-not-go-to-Ger-ma-ny."

As soon as the factories let out, they would be in the bistros talking about it, bistros where they knew the owner was not with the police and where they could talk without having to be afraid. They felt free. Still free to choose between going and refusing to go. Free to act according to what their conscience alone told them to do. As free as they had been back in the day, when they would have decided to go on strike, pitting their power against the power of the oppressor who had learned over time to see them as a force to be reckoned with.

This was the first time since the armistice that the choice to act was theirs,[2] even if that choice meant no action or refusal.

"You know," one of them said, "if I could go replace my cousin who is more like a brother to me, if I could say, I'm more than willing to go as long as you release my cousin Merlin (first name Marcel) who is like a brother to me, in that case, I would go."

"Absolutely," they agreed.

---

2. The armistice of June 1940. Hitler insisted on signing it in the same railway car that the November 1918 armistice of World War I had been signed in.

Another said: "Yes, but being able to get someone else released would be worth it, even if it couldn't be somebody you knew."

Everyone took the guy who said that for a good kid. He was not a police informer or a scab, for sure. But he lacked drive. During the strikes of '36, the most he would say was: "If that's how you all see it." Then he would join them on the march. His brother was a gardener for the Marchioness of Loctudy, as his father was, as it had always been in their family, the job passed down from father to son. He believed that he must carry out God's will and that the will of men is not always God's will, the proof being that God had created the poor and the rich—the people who work and the people they worked for, as it was in the beginning and ever shall be. Rich and powerful people retain the power of God, insofar as they are rich and powerful, which they would not be without God's will. With his wife dying of tuberculosis in the Laennec Hospital and his children all dead at a very young age, the only thing he, Le Guirrec, had to do was obey the rich and powerful, since, as all evidence showed, misery and lowliness were God's will for him. And now the only thing he had to do was obey the Maréchal.[3]

3. Referring to Pétain. Though Pétain's title, *maréchal*, is often translated as "marshal," this term does not have an equivalent in English. In France, *maréchal* is a military honor, not a military rank. Pétain was granted the

"But you're obeying German orders," the others objected, knowing Le Guirrec was at least as French and as Breton as he was Catholic.

"I believe in obeying the Maréchal," he obstinately replied; "the Maréchal knows what he's doing."

Nevertheless, Le Guirrec did not go: he could not leave his wife to die alone in the hospital. He could not leave his home. By that, did he mean his shambles of a room—too small to be orderly—with its view of the smokestacks, the tin roofs, and the train tracks? Or did he mean that plot of land his family had lived on and worked for centuries now but still did not own? Or was it his language, which they did not speak here either.[4] Still, this was his home.

And Le Guirrec was not leaving.

There were those two who had signed up for Germany, both very young and full of ideas. They had no convictions; they were not out to "save Europe from Bolshevism." Bolshevism meant nothing to them. What they

distinction for his military performance in World War I. Tried and sentenced to death for treason after World War II, he was stripped of all military ranks and honors, except for that of *maréchal*. Because of Pétain's age (ninety at the time of his trial), President Charles de Gaulle commuted Pétain's sentence to life in prison.

4. The Jules Ferry laws of 1881 and 1882, lauded for making elementary education in France compulsory, free, and nonreligious, also banned all languages but French from the classroom, at a time when millions of children in France spoke only the language of their region. For decades after, children were humiliated and punished for speaking the only language they knew (e.g., Breton or Basque) when at school.

saw was an opportunity for adventure, a free ride they could not refuse. Freeloaders were not the type of people to be trusted. On top of that, they were mediocre workers, more like handymen in fact. Better off without them. Guys like that would hardly be contributing to Germany's victory.

The newspapers, however, kept touting the great success of the relief program, saying that trains were departing for Germany every day. But here they knew for a fact that only two workers had signed up on their own initiative. And that out of more than a thousand of them, only twenty-five had gone to the conference organized by management, and even then, only after they had agreed with all the others to come back with a precise account of what had been said there. With that being the case here, there was no reason to believe the program had made a different impression anywhere else, or that their buddies at the Renault factory or at Gnome and Rhône were any more inclined to go to Germany than they were.[5]

In fact, they soon noticed that the appeals were getting more insistent, that "volunteers" were being assigned and called mandatory volunteers (in the same way Europe now meant Germany; socialism, the dictatorship of corporate interests; and food provision, organized starvation:

5. Gnome et Rhône was a major aircraft engine manufacturer in France.

it did not take a scholar to know that the meanings of words had changed and had to be taken as the reverse of what you once thought they meant).

"So what will you do if you get the order?" they asked each other for the umpteenth time.

"I won't leave."

"Easy to say, but where will you go?"

And that was the real question. Maybe they would go meet up with de Gaulle?[6] There was talk of trawlers leaving the ports with a certain number of men and returning with the same number, only the faces were different. The exchange took place with British ships out at sea. What about heading for the free zone and enrolling in the armistice army? The armistice army, what a joke, run by all those generals who had never before received anything close to the attention they got once they had been defeated: the bourgeoisie's triumphant, defeated armistice army. Anyway, that army had been disbanded, and now the "free" zone was occupied. The only thing left to do

---

6. Virtually unheard of in France when he was stationed in London and recognized by Britain as leader of the Forces Françaises Libres (Free French Forces) in 1940, General Charles de Gaulle first became familiar to the French as a voice on the BBC's Radio Londres (Radio London) exhorting the French to resist Nazi occupation. Besides boosting French morale and countering the onslaught of Nazi propaganda on Radio Paris and Radio Vichy, Radio Londres transmitted hundreds of coded messages that aided de Gaulle in coordinating the Free French and Allied interventions from outside France with the growing Resistance within France.

was hide out here in the countryside, and wait for weapons. But you needed to know people in the countryside.

*

Robert Basin was wondering yet again: So what am I going to do now?

He had been asking himself that question all day long, as he stood before a lathe that did not sound good. Here or over there, what did it matter, you were working for the Germans just the same.

Now that the factory had let out for the day, his thoughts returned to the question as he rested his elbows on the bridge railing, the Seine crawling along beneath him. At Renault, smokestacks stood prow-like despite last year's bombing, full steam ahead on a voyage to nowhere. Across the river, the Sèvres hills led up to a man-made forest that no one could hide in.

What am I going to do now?

He felt around in his pocket for the order to report to the Gare de l'Est.[7] The folded piece of paper was still there. He wanted to chuck it into the river. That would be that, and he would see what happened next. He spat into the water.

The reasons for staying that the workers had been tossing around for days on end did not convince him, because

7. Gare de l'Est is the main station in Paris for trains going eastward.

none of them truly believed he would be the one to get the departure order. As in the thought process where you believed you would win the lottery because you had bought a ticket, they never really thought anything bad would happen to them personally. That was how people managed to go on living despite the evidence. He would have to go over all of it again, applying it directly to himself this time.

At first, he had no doubts about choosing not to go. I am working for them here too, that much is obvious: all of Europe is working for them. But I do no more than what it takes not to get fired. Not to mention all those parts with their practically undetectable defects. Now that was a job well done. Besides, if they want to send us to Germany, it's because they believe it is in their best interest: either they believe they can get more work out of us over there, and then use us as soldiers, or they want to round out the haul they made in 1940 to rid France of anyone capable of pointing a weapon in their direction. Whatever the reason, and maybe all are valid, if it is in their interest, then we have to do the exact opposite. Therefore, I must not go. I must not go.

But he kept hearing that question: "What will you do if you're called up?"

He saw Le Guirrec coming his way, Le Guirrec who had also received his departure order that morning.

Wanting to avoid him, Robert went on across the bridge. Not that Le Guirrec had noticed him anyway: the man often walked as if he carried the weight of the world on his shoulders.

"So what will you do if you're called up?"

Simone was supposed to be home by now, though they made her work extra hours virtually every day.

As soon as she opened the door to let him in, she knew: "You're leaving," she said.

Below her eyes her face was drawn, like it always was in the evening after a long day of work had exhausted her.

"I got my orders," he responded in a neutral voice.

"You mustn't leave," she said.

But he did not know if he was supposed to refuse so as not to assist in Hitler's subjugation of Europe or because he loved her: she made everything even more confusing. He did know that since he had met her, he had become a better person. And if he had to explain what he meant by "better," he would say he felt more aware, more personally responsible for things.

She got undressed and stretched out naked on the bed. And now he was going to join her. Just a man and a naked woman, for all eternity.

"Don't leave," she repeated.

She wrapped her arms around his neck the way women do. He let her do it.

"Don't leave," she said for the third time.

She curled up next to him, nestled between the hollow of his shoulder and his hip.

"How can I avoid it?" he asked.

"I'll hide you," she answered.

And true enough, Simone was his home.

"But where?" he asked.

There was only the one room with a toilet next to it.

"Who will know you're here?" she persisted. "I'll say we had a fight and you left me."

She snuggled up to him even closer, trying to ward off the destiny her very words might bring about.

"What about my provisions card?"

"I'll take care of that. I'll try to hide you in the countryside. I'll tell my aunt you're my fiancé."—Immediately she wished she hadn't said that: he must not feel tied down by her. "She has a little farm in the middle of the woods, three structures out there in the woods."

He would entrust himself to this woman, his woman, to her words that wrapped around him, calm and confident in the steadfast complicity of home.

"Some men have to stay here," she went on, as if trying to respond to an objection he had not raised, an objection to softness and cowardice, to taking the easy way out. "When the time comes for rifles and machine guns, that's when you will go, and I will not stop you."

Night Watch

The wind has picked up from the west, and a full moon gallops behind the clouds above. Trees arch their naked backs along both sides of the road. All is movement and stillness.

A door, opened just long enough to reveal a glowing fireplace, slams shut. Then darkness engulfs the village once more, the darkness of "caves and swamps,"[1] darker

1. "Des cavernes et des marécages" in the French. Given how Thomas juxtaposes hearth light, electricity (representing scientific progress), and the courthouse (justice) against the threatening darkness (the Nazi occupation), the likely source for the quotation is André Lefèvre's *La philosophie* (*Philosophy*; C. Reinwald, 1879), a massive history of human knowledge. In it, the phrase "des cavernes et des marécages" conjures a primitive time when humankind "ne connaissait . . . ni famille, ni societé, ni justice" ("did not know family, society or justice"; 175). Lefèvre continues: "Le foyer, créateur des arts et de la civilisation, devint le centre sacré de la famille" ("The hearth, creator of arts and civilization, became the sacred center of the family"; 175–76; my trans.), on which society was founded. In the 1880s, Lefèvre was a better-known member of the freethinkers movement, which championed scientific knowledge as key to establishing and maintaining a democratic, egalitarian, and just society. Jennifer Hecht's *The End of the Soul: Scientific Modernity, Atheism, and Anthropology in France* (Columbia UP, 2003) includes a chapter on this little-studied movement (257–95), which would have influenced French leftist intellectuals like Thomas.

still after the brief illumination. Electric lampposts with their burned-out bulbs stand guard around the unlit courthouse. The posts went up just before the war: for six months you could see the road at night. No longer visible, it runs beneath the galloping moon, across the vast expanse of Europe and toward the East, where there is light because villages are on fire.

Wooden shoes come clomping down the road, against the wind, peaceful shoes for peaceful times. Another door opens to warmth and light.

"Evening, Jean, evening, Marie."

"Evening, Appolonie."

"Shhhh, don't make any noise."

Leaving her wooden shoes at the door, the old woman slides on a pair of slippers and goes to hunch over the wireless radio.[2]

They are holding onto a long cable with one end planted in a bucket of water. They do this in order to tune in to stations secretly broadcasting beneath the babble of enemy music. This is London. This is Moscow. This is Algiers. And through Algiers, this is America. And thus, news from the around the world comes whispering into their closed room.

2. German policy made owning or listening to a radio, particularly one tuned to a non-German radio station, punishable by death.

In this faraway village, tucked in among the surrounding woods and hills, you might believe you are living in a safe, self-sufficient place, a place war cannot touch, since war cannot change the seasons. You might believe that. And that is what they would like us to believe. In the papers, they love to go on about the happy nostalgia of the countryside and the ancient wisdom of peasant folk, and to preach about a "return to the land"—source of all wealth, peace, and truth. But here, we know what the real story is. We know that opportunities in the cities have been drawing people away for decades, and sometimes some of them get lucky. They are drawn to the movement and light and adventure of city life, as inevitably as plants turn toward the sun. We also know that the houses here are meager and tumbling down as the manure keeps piling up just outside their front doors. We know that tomorrow will be exactly like today and that people here will die as they were born, with no idea that life is what happens between birth and death. Just as it was for my father and my grandfather. So what's the use of my being born here when life plays out and change happens somewhere else? And as for that peasant wisdom, well, there is old Chambert, who got back at his neighbor by burning down his haystack after he refused to sell a plot of land that bordered on Chambert's . . .

"Listen, we've got London."

. . . But we also know we are part of all that goes on in this world, even if a blackbird's singing can make us forget that momentarily.

We all move closer to the wireless radio that our destiny depends on, knowing this war is indeed going to change our lives here.

But Appolonie is thinking about her son who will never come home. Her husband was killed too, in the other war. So will there always be war, until the end of time? Or will we someday learn how to build a world without war? But that won't bring Appolonie's son back to her, that unique individual her son was and never will be again . . .

Jean turned a knob on the radio, and the voice came back.

But peacetime is a woman's dream; it has to be conquered, taken by force. Anyway, this is neither a time of peace nor one of war for us, but some imprecise, nameless time. His rifle is buried in the back of the garden. He'll have to go out and oil it before the rust sets in. He doesn't feel hatred. When he left for this war, he didn't feel hatred for the men lying low across the Rhine, just like the men over here were doing. But for what those men were defending and were forced to want to impose on the world, and have imposed on us here, and for their known complicity—for those things, yes, he feels hatred. And for all the long days and months of waiting that have rattled people's courage, magnified their apprehension, and insinuated and then crystallized their sense of betrayal. Why, for all these long months, did we have to watch German planes fly over our landing fields after we had been given orders not to fire on them? Why, for all these long months, have they only found the time to set up the markers for building a line of defense out in the Frévillard forest, while we sit here unemployed? For all of this, yes, he feels hatred. But he knows his rifle is hidden in the back of the garden. And he knows why he hid it there. And he knows that from one village to the next, there are others like him, just waiting for the signal . . .

. . . Where does he go at night, Marie wonders, off on his bicycle like that and not coming home until morning? Or not coming home at all, but heading straight to work instead? After all, he promised that the story with the redhead was over and that I was the only woman for him. So where can he be spending the night when he doesn't come home until morning, soaked through to the skin with mist and dew? And I'm the one who has to have a clean shirt ready for him and to start the fire so he can get warm and have his coffee. Who would do that for him if I didn't? And why do I have to be the one who loves him, so madly that I wait up for him all night long?

She's watching him. He's bent over the wireless. She sees his tense face, all its angles magnified in the fireplace light. All the lines on his forehead. And all of her happiness, all of her desperation, inscribed on his forehead, her life and death contained in his body. She feels her own existence solely through his; and she knows that right now she does not exist for him, that he, in turn, exists only through the distant, scrambled murmur of the magical voices coming in directly from London, Moscow, Algiers . . . I may be losing my mind.

She'd like to go and lay her forehead on his knees, in passionate, complete submission to him. But what would old Appolonie think, seeing her bowed down before him like a slave from ancient history, Appolonie who is always telling her: "You're crazy, my child, worse than a cat. Come on now, no man is worth crying over. Unless, of course, he's your son. Not unless he's your son."

The radio has gone silent. "Tell me what they said," Appolonie says. "My hearing isn't so good today."

Marie leans in to listen too: Stalingrad will not be taken by the Germans because, by holding out against their assailants for months upon months, the Russians have now broken the enemy down. That is Stalingrad to the east, so far away that the wind from here loses strength en route and dies out before it ever gets there. Stalingrad, where each home is a fortress, every street a trench.

"The Russians are showing us we need to know how to fight, and how to die."

Who is talking about dying tonight?

Appolonie has opened the door. A quick rush of wind rousts the flame in the fireplace. You can hear her wooden shoes clomping across the courtyard.

Marie turns back around and all the color, except for the mauve of her eyelids, drains from her face when she sees him reach for his leather jacket.

"You're leaving again tonight?"

Forehead creased in irritation, he doesn't reply. She knows if she tries to hold him back, he'll only push her away.

She hears him getting his bicycle out of the shed. And after that, nothing more . . .

Lime Blossom Tea

"They" had occupied "the Chateau" from the beginning.

From her concierge quarters she watched them come and go, all day long amid a racket of boots and motors and marching songs. The first time she saw them change guard, in that goose-stepping ceremony they do, she thought she might die laughing (if she had felt like laughing, but she hardly ever did). One day, a soldier had gone to take his post—one, two, one, two—and, lifting his leg very high and stiffly, had fallen down just as he went to turn. At that point she did laugh, all alone in her satisfaction, and was very happy to see that they saw her laughing. But an officer had kicked the soldier several times while he was still lying on the ground. The soldier got up, bright red, and stood there at attention while the officer gave him what for in a language she did not understand. But one did not need to understand. And she was overcome with pity. Yes, she felt some kind of pity for the soldier. Then those soldiers left, and others came in their place. But that racket of boots and motors and marching songs was always the same.

For a few months, no soldiers showed up. The country folk kept asking her: "So, have your potato bugs left?"[1] To be sure, they still occupied France, but the fact that they were no longer in the vicinity was a great relief to everyone. At that point, Old Lady Renaude decided to put a little order back into the chateau "so Monsieur wouldn't have to see it like this if he came back."

The studs of the soldiers' boots had gouged the parquet floors, and all the rosewood dining room chairs had been broken. One morning, she found the books from the library strewn across the great lawn in front of the house. It had rained, and they were all water-damaged. Old Lady Renaude did not understand much about books, but she knew that Monsieur always had his nose stuck in one. That is why she had carefully gathered them up and placed them in the other room of her quarters, where she stored her honey, her nuts, and her apples.

She spent a good month hanging all the clothing back up in the armoires, washing the windowpanes, and mending the curtains. Just when things were beginning to feel more settled, the soldiers returned. Old Lady Renaude could have cried over all the trouble she had gone to for nothing.

---

1. In French, a *doryphore* is a type of potato beetle. In the occupied zone, the French came to equate German soldiers with *doryphores* because both were so numerous and both depleted the potato supply.

But there was just a small group of them. And they explained—the short one spoke French fairly well—that they were there just to guard the rail bridge that crossed the river at the far end of the park. And she replied, "Good, good," to cut it short. She was not about to get into a conversation with them now, was she? Then she dropped the bundle of grass she had been carrying on her back, letting out a little groan as she did so. And the soldier said to her: "Allow me, *Matame*."

He grabbed the bundle and took it clear across the park and up to the rabbit hutches.

The following day he saw her going down to the field, scythe and canvas bag in hand. He took them from her and went to cut the grass himself. And now each day, at the same time, he came to get the scythe and the bag so he could cut the grass. There was also a tall blond soldier who would go to the fountain and fill her pail with water. He spoke no French at all. He could only say "Grandmother"—the one word the other guy had taught him—as he patted her on the head. And true enough, her hair was all white, and with each passing day, she looked more and more like an old woman. They were good boys.

So she had been wondering what she could do for them. She saw them mending their own socks. Any way you slice it, a man holding a needle is a pitiful sight. Even when that man is an enemy and in your home. She set about mending their socks.

In the village they would ask: "Old Lady Renaude, are you turning into a collaborator?"

She defended herself. They were good boys, that was all. And if you had to live side by side with them every day, what would you do? No, of course she did not like their Hitler, or the Maréchal, or Monsieur Laval. Especially not Laval![2] She had even torn up the Maréchal's portrait, which she had bought early on when they were told it had to be on display in their homes. So there you have it.

Autumn arrived with the thick mists that rise in the morning, hang low over the river until about ten, then suddenly break to make way for the sun, and with the night that falls early, night in its purest form, come to warn those least prepared that winter is on its way.

Hans often hung around in the evenings; he liked being near her under the lamplight. If only she were ten years younger and did not have the white hair that made them call her "grandmother." In truth, she was only forty-

2. In contrast to how they viewed Pétain, the French overwhelmingly despised Pierre Laval, who served briefly in 1940 as vice president of the Council of State before being ousted. He returned with Nazi support in April 1942 as minister of foreign affairs, information, and the interior. Like Pétain, Laval was charged with treason after the war, but unlike Pétain, Laval was executed.

five, but many would say that she looked ten years older. Regardless, she was old enough to be his mother . . .

He was coughing one day, and she said, "Wait, I'm going to make you a cup of lime blossom tea," because it made her happy to do something his own mother would have done for him. She went into the adjacent room to get the honey she kept on hand for winter colds. Offering him a silver spoon that dated back to her wedding, she said: "Take as much as you'd like to sweeten your tea."

And now he was licking the spoon like a little boy.

"I haven't eaten honey in ages," he said. "Back home in Germany, only capitalists can afford to buy it. Capitalism there is even worse than it is here."

Old Lady Renaude was not quite sure what "capitalism" meant. All she knew was that it existed in France and Germany because Hans had said so.

"Hitler rescued capitalism for our country. And we are rescuing it for yours. Here's what I think about Hitler."

He spat into the fire, making it hiss. "That's what I think about him," he repeated.

"Then why did you make him your leader?" asked Old Lady Renaude.

"And what about you, why do you have your Maréchal?" retorted Hans. "Because you were defeated, that's why."

"But you are the victors," said Old Lady Renaude.

"We were defeated," said Hans, "on 30 January 1933."

Old Lady Renaude did not know what had happened on 30 January 1933.[3] And she did not ask. Hans kept on talking, his eyes completely focused on the fire, as if he could see what he was describing, there in the fire.

And in the fire, dark settlements on the outskirts of a major city appeared, where all the household and factory waste had been piling up and apparently had to remain. And in the fire appeared all those men and women camped out in huts made of mud brick and plaster debris, who were tolerated because the factories might require their labor. And in the fire appeared those who were crammed together in the huge, smoke-blackened barracks that served as factory housing. Utter hopelessness. They'd found no work for years after the other war, only unemployment and hunger.

When he was a little boy, Hans used to follow the processions through the streets, red flags flapping in the wind, big banners calling for a more human life. For Hans, that meant having bread every day, with some butter sometimes, or some jam. And a set of lead soldiers like the one he saw at the Friedrichstrasse bazaar. For a ten-year-old, such things make life more human.

Mother would say, "This little boy is going to get hurt," then furiously to her husband: "I already have enough to

3. The date Hitler was named chancellor of Germany.

worry about with you!" Hans remembered men coming to their house late in the evening after work. Once they had eaten, they would huddle in close around the table. They kept their voices low and spoke quickly. Hans could not make out what they were saying. His father would look up and say: "Hans, go into the other room; you don't need to be in here." Hans did not like the other room because it had no windows. It was not actually a room; it was a dark storage closet. He would find his mother in there, sitting on a crate and sobbing: "This is all going to turn out very badly."

They now knew they could not trust the gas company service manager who lived a few houses over. Mother used to clean for him, but Father had put a stop to that. And they could not trust the household goods representative from the second floor. They could not say anything in front of either neighbor because both were Nazis: they saw them parading around on Sundays in their brand-new uniforms. The boys had started playing Nazis and Communists in the streets. Hans never wanted to play a Nazi.

Father would come home in the evenings more worried than ever. He would say: "Kaufmann and Hübner just got caught." Mother would beg him: "Please stop this. You're tempting God." He would shrug his shoulders: "I can't stop now, people are depending on me."

The days passed, and Father was still a free man, because neither Kaufmann nor Hübner had given up any names. Little by little they started hearing about what was going on in the prisons and the camps. About the torture . . .

Hans fell silent, his eyes still on the fire. Old Lady Renaude removed her glasses and said: "Things like that aren't possible here in France."

"Things like that are possible anywhere," said Hans. "And here too, Hitler will find men who will do those things. He will find them," he insisted.

The fire crackled. You could hear an owl hooting in the woods nearby. Night had fallen completely.

"One day, around four in the morning, there was a knock at the door. I can still hear my father saying: 'Don't open it.' Those are the last words I ever heard my father say. I remember the tone he used when he said them. But the knocking got louder: 'Open up, police,' someone shouted. Then: 'If you don't open up, we'll arrest your wife and your son too.' So my father went to the door and he opened it.

"The policemen searched everywhere. They found nothing. My mother stood in a corner, crying. Then they took my father away. We found out that he and several others had been shot a few days later."

"My poor boy," Old Lady Renaude whispered.

"They tried to make us believe that they were speaking on behalf of the German people, that their only concern was for the good of the German community. German youths were required to enroll in camps that, they claimed, would turn us all into well-trained animals. And there were many who, on account of being compelled to commit certain acts, wound up believing that they carried them out freely and of their own accord. Because she would go and beg for clothing at the Winter Relief office, my mother wound up believing it was good to be a beggar. What I remembered was my father's death. I managed to get hold of all the banned books he had read. I learned to understand my father's death. It's the only hope we have left of being saved. And maybe the only one you have left as well."

The Escapees

In the middle of the woods, among pine and birch trees, there is a perfectly squared-off field. The birch leaves tremble constantly, even when there is no wind.

A wide swath of fading sky stretches out across other fields that have been cleared of their wood. Ever trembling, the silvery birch leaves glint in the setting sun.

A man is hunched over, pulling stumps from land hemmed in by the woods for so long that it holds onto roots as if they were coiled snakes or a disease.

The man lifts his hoe, brings it down on a root, removes the root with some difficulty, and tosses it aside. He stops for a moment and raises his sweaty face. The birch leaves carry on with their trembling.

Two men, pale with exhaustion, appear at the edge of the woods. Looking around, they see the man clearing stumps from the field in the middle of the woods. They walk up to him.

"Hello," they say.

"Hello," the man replies.

"Do you know if there's a spring nearby?" they ask. "We haven't had any water since this morning."

And just then, the man hears the burbling spring, which he had not heard until that moment, because for days on end he has been so focused on pulling stumps that he stopped hearing the familiar sounds around him.

"That way," says the man.

They kneel down at the spring's edge. Water pours into a stone trough from a pipe jutting out of the embankment. It must have been built a long time ago, when there was a village nearby; you can still see its vestiges. First they drink the water from their hands. Then they put their heads under the falling water, still drinking it in as it washes the thick dust from their faces. Then they slick back their hair and, despite being unshaven, look the way they used to look: two very young men, practically still boys.

The man immediately understood who they were. This used to be the route for religious pilgrimages; now it was used by escapees.

"By the way," they ask, "is there somewhere can we sleep tonight?"

The man points downhill toward a smoking chimney surrounded by rooftops of barns and stables.

"Are they good Frenchmen?" they ask.

"Yes, they're good Frenchmen. Tell them you were sent by Martin, the guy clearing stumps up the hill."

They head off, trudging along in their clodhoppers. Every once in a while, a loosened rock rolls down the path and breaks apart.

The birch leaves tremble.

A dog pulls on his chain and barks. Chickens cackle around a pile of manure. The two men head straight for the door, only the top part of which is open. They knock. A very young woman with curly hair appears. She could well be the first French woman they have seen in ages. They ask: "Can we sleep here in the barn?"

And she replies: "I'll fix up two beds for you in the grain store. We haven't harvested yet so there's room for you in there."

She can tell these young men are not vagrants, not homeless wanderers who act like they are looking for work but don't really want to find any, who take off the moment you say: "Stay, we have plenty of work for you here." These days, anybody can become a vagrant, just like that, including my brother, who is a prisoner, or us, tomorrow, if a bomb falls on the farm, and if we have to leave again, like we did during the exodus.[1]

1. This "exodus" refers to the mass movement of populations—some two million from Belgium, Luxembourg, and Holland, another two million from northern France, and two million more from Paris—toward the south of France in May and June 1940, where they sought safety from the invading German army.

Personally, I'm not leaving this time. I would rather die here.

And now, seated at the brown table, they are eating a real meal, the first one in years. Yes, indeed, it has been years since they have eaten an omelet like this, with bacon and this kind of bread.

One by one, they are back from the fields: the Boss, the Farmhand, Joseph the Cart Driver, and even Martin, who is always late, as if something up there held him back, something he had a hard time leaving. But there was nothing to look at up there, so who knows what it could have been, unless it was the birch leaves.

First came the marching: if exhaustion brought you down, a rifle butt got you back up, until the exhaustion knocked you down again. A guy right next to me died from it. I couldn't do anything to help him.

Then the endless days and the slowness and lethargy of the camps. Waiting for food, waiting for letters, waiting for packages, waiting for the day to be over, waiting for news that never came, and still, you had to get up the next morning, even though you knew the day would only bring more waiting.

Then they made them board a train. Through the barred windows of the livestock car, they watched a vast, deserted terrain pass them by: a sprawling plain that went on forever and that had patches of snow here and there even though it was the end of April, twisted junipers, a wide expanse of sad earth, and an endless gray sky above. Then the plain stopped at a train station, and they saw a woman gesturing to them from her window. She went away for a moment and came back holding a big piece of cardboard that read: "People of France, you are in Poland. We will do whatever we can to help you." Then the woman disappeared and the plain started rolling along again. Further and further eastward, further and further away, as if they were never going to stop.

For months on end, they worked on fortifications. But in the evenings as they returned to the camp, stiff and exhausted, children would sneak up to them along the way and give them food, even though they hardly had anything to eat themselves. Thus they kept the woman's welcome promise. Thus it went for months. And it was during that time that the two young men met and promised each other they would always stick together.

The faucet on the kitchen sink was dripping. From outside, not a sound. But in here, scenes of a suffering Europe at war were unfolding.

"In Germany, we worked in a factory. We were not allowed to talk to German civilians. But the foreman, on the pretext of explaining our jobs to us, came by each day to give us the news from the British radio station, remember that, Jean? He would say: 'When you get back to

France, you must tell them that not all of us are behind Hitler. You must tell them . . .' Remember that, Jean?"

And now they felt it was their duty to repeat religiously what the German foreman told them to say. The others, Martin and Joseph, and the Boss, shook their heads: so if they were fed up with their Hitler, why was the war lasting so long?

They heard the telephone ring. The woman got up, and when she came back she was very pale:

"They're calling from Les Charmettes," she said. "They've had a visit from the police because of that ox hide someone found buried in the forest . . . The police are on their way. They're coming here."[2]

They hurried the young men across the courtyard. The rising moon shone down on the pond below. From high above, a nightingale sang. They pushed the young men into a little barn that smelled of dry hay.

"We'll come back for you as soon as the danger has passed," said the Boss.

And they shut the door behind them.

The two young men stretched out side by side on the hay, as they had been doing for months. They were not afraid; it did not seem like anything would ever happen

2. The mention of an ox hide implies that the police are looking for poachers.

to them again. Tomorrow they would be home. Their adventure was coming to an end.

"Do you think we might actually miss this?" one of them asked.

This was not a question he would have dared to ask until now. Even now, it sounded sacrilegious. And in the complete darkness that surrounded them, the other responded: "Will we ever be able to return to this life?"

And suddenly, he was overcome with an unspeakable tenderness and an indescribable malaise as he thought about the corner of the living room where his mother sat knitting and sipping her tea. Something had ended for him: the time from before, the boy he used to be. But then he had not yet known this other, who had been born since.

And from up above, higher still, the nightingale sang.

The Arrest

Her mother opened her eyes, a faint smile appearing on her lips. For just that moment the face that had been wearing a death mask returned to life. Then she closed her eyes again. But from somewhere deep within, she had signaled that she was still alive and that she would live.

Anne almost fell to her knees at the foot of the bed to thank someone, something, God. But if she was supposed to thank God for her mother's resurrection, for this happy event she had just experienced herself, then she also had to blame God for the horrific world they were living in, for each individual tragedy that was experienced at any given moment and that collectively constituted a shared tragedy, for all the world's suffering and all its pathetic happiness. Above men, there existed no being she could thank for her joy without also holding it responsible for the suffering. If such a being did exist, if it were endowed with a conscience and reason, it could only be a capricious, childish monster. It made no sense to attribute all that is good to God and then to let him off the hook for all that is evil simply by declaring his ways unfathomable.

The existence of evil sufficed to negate God, and this negation was God's only excuse. She thought she had put such pointless pondering to rest a long time ago. But because of this moment of happiness—this unexpected happiness—here it was, resurfacing again. Conscience, like the earth, had its geological layers, each of a different age.

She sat down by her mother's bed and tried to take her mother's hand without moving it, as if she feared scaring off this unique, reawakening life. She felt the skin of her mother's hand, warm, soft, and alive beneath her own. She kissed the thin, veiny wrist. "My poor mother," she murmured, her eyes filling with tears of gratitude.

The surgeon came in.

"She opened her eyes," said Anne.

He smiled: "I told you I would save her."

This man could do no harm. She felt close to him, filled with confidence in this man's knowledge. And in humankind. But then her thoughts suddenly turned to all the young people dying *at this very minute*. Nothing made any sense.

She sat with her hand placed over her mother's for a while. Daylight glided across the room's white walls. From the sun's position, she knew she would not be able to stay much longer. She had been granted a moment of reprieve, but soon she would have to get back to her task.

Suddenly, she heard footsteps advancing down the hall, the heavy sound that boots make. Her mother's room was at the very end of the hall. The boots were coming closer. Now she *knew* the boots were coming for her. Was she afraid? Being afraid meant consenting to her fear, not feeling it. She had always been the kind of person for whom it was easier to refuse than to surrender, easier to rebel than to accept. She was about to find out what she was really made of.

Someone opened the door without knocking. She *knew* what would be behind the door, and there stood two Germans in uniform. The face of the nurse, Mademoiselle Benizat, appeared behind them, pale beneath her nurse's cap. Anne could see one of her eyes widen beneath an arched brow. I am calm, she told herself, because I can notice a tiny detail like that. I am completely calm. But her legs had gone weak. I wonder if I will be able to walk.

"Anne Roger," one of the Germans demanded in a heavy accent.

"Yes," she said, rising to her feet. Her legs had gone weak, but they could still support her. Now she was standing before them—very small in comparison, but ready to take them on, which is easier to do standing up than sitting down.

"Please follow us," they said.

They were perfectly polite. She could allow neither their politeness nor their threats to have any effect on her. She had entered an unfamiliar terrain of hunter and hunted, where any kind of ruse or trap was fair play.

"Where?" she asked.

"To your house," they said.

She turned around and saw her mother's eyes wide upon her, her thin neck strained beyond capacity to raise her head from her pillow. Anne's mouth trembled.

"At least let me give my mother a kiss."

She bent down and touched her lips to her mother's cold, damp forehead.

"Calm down," she said aloud, "there's nothing at all in my apartment. I'll come right back. Mademoiselle Benizat," she added, "would you be kind enough to make up a bed for me for this evening, here in my mother's room?"

Then she left with the soldiers. She had no difficulty walking, or crossing the landing where housekeepers and nurses and the assistant furtively appeared. She greeted them.

She had no difficulty going down the stairs, or getting into the car that was waiting for them. She had not been in a car for months. Two pigeons were pecking about on the sidewalk. Within an instant, Anne was able to distinguish all the various shades of gray in their feathers: mouse gray, slate gray, sky gray, smoke gray, and a gray verging on russet, like the color of old roof tiles under the sun.

"This may be the last time I ever see pigeons," she said to herself. Then she thought about her mother, and it felt as if her heart had grown too large for her chest. *As long as I don't cry.* That was the last thing she needed. She had held herself together so far, but this was only the beginning.

The housekeeper came and opened the door.

"Oh! Mademoiselle," she cried, "How is your . . . ?"

Then Anne saw the housekeeper's face stricken with terror.

They all went inside. The Germans asked where her office was, and she led them to her bedroom. She watched them open all her drawers and throw their contents out on the rug. From time to time, they would focus on a piece of paper, read it carefully, then toss it out with the rest. She knew they would not find anything; even if they turned her apartment inside out, they would never find anything they were looking for. Now she felt sure of herself, that she would yield no more information than her apartment had; she felt like herself again, pure and self-controlled, passionately self-controlled.

Then it was time to go through all the books in her library. "You have a number of works by Karl Marx," they remarked.

"And I have Nietzsche, and Plato, and Kierkegaard," she responded.

They shook the books open, then threw them on the floor along with her stockings and her dresses. For two hours they carried on with their crude task. They were conscientious men who did their job conscientiously.

"Putting all this stuff back where it belongs is going to be such a chore!" muttered the housekeeper who came in from time to time to take a look.

Anne found the housekeeper's comment ridiculous. She wondered why and discovered that the answer lay in the disproportion between the consequences the housekeeper imagined and what they were really going to be. Obviously the machine was working.

The Germans' search had finally reached its end. They went back into the living room, told her to sit down, and took a seat themselves. This is no longer my home. Now it is theirs. She took on her role, sitting politely as a visitor. It was no longer up to her belongings to withhold information; it was up to her. She had known how to arrange for the things around her to keep silent. Would she be able to remain so herself? They began to interrogate her.

Did she know Z, a professor at ______________? Yes, she knew him. He was an old friend of her father's. Well, he had just been arrested. And he was talking.

"Talking about what?" she asked. "I don't understand."

The fact that Z had been arrested was a terrible blow. For him first of all. And then for the others. And then for herself. But he will hold out, she told herself. And like a boxer used to taking blows, she felt herself taking charge of the situation. She was ready for the next round.

She saw herself seated on the chair, responding to their questions as if she were both on stage and in the audience at the same time. Thank goodness, she thought, that she had always "played a role" throughout her life and had forced herself to play it well, never tolerating anything in herself not suitable to that role, and that she had worked so hard to be like the person she had chosen to be and had thus over time become: the type who would not allow contempt to get the best of her.

She heard herself deny, deny, deny, the easiest defense (and the one best suited to her sincerity, because the role generates a certain way of being sincere). No, she was not involved in any political activity. No, she was not involved in anything. No, she did not know what they were talking about. No, she had never heard anything about that plot, or those meetings, or those tracts.

The face of the man interrogating her appeared inordinately large from across the table. She could see the wrinkles on his reddish skin and big pores along the sides of his nose and on his cheeks. His unseeing eyes were green globes streaked with tiny darker veins, as expressionless as two aquamarine marbles. No. No. No. The other one had a long, pendulous, hairless chin that he held in his hand as if he feared he might lose it. And all the while, she could hear herself playing the witless, naive woman who kept saying no.

"Very well," said the man with the hairless chin, who up to that point had not uttered a word. "We will have other ways of making you talk."

"Please follow us," he added politely.

Then she remembered her mother, the big, vulnerable eyes of her emaciated face, the bluish wrist at the end of her skeletal arm. I will never see her again. Anne got a lump in her throat. Was it fear? Was it grief? She had chosen to deny everything.

"May I have a word with the housekeeper?" she asked.

"In front of us," they said.

Mariette was sitting on a stool in the kitchen. When they came in, she started to shake so badly you could hear her teeth rattle.

"Mariette," said Anne, "please go to the clinic right away and tell Mother that there's nothing to worry about. These gentlemen will release me as soon as they realize they have made a mistake."

She kissed Mariette on the cheek. This may be the last time I ever give anyone a kiss.

Then she walked out the front door, her heels resounding every bit as loudly as the boot steps of the Germans.

FTP

The French struck with heart and vigor.

—*The Song of Roland*

He was told: "A train of German soldiers is coming through tonight at 11:34."[1]

From the station it takes less than five minutes to reach the forest. So they can expect the German train at 11:39. He went to the little bistro near the station anyway, where René usually has lunch. Sure enough, René was there in the corner eating with the stationmaster. He walked over to the table. They exchanged casual greetings and talked about the weather.

---

1. The Francs-Tireurs et Partisans (Partisan Irregular Riflemen; FTP) was a resistance group established in 1941 as the military branch of the French Communist Party (but was open to non-Communists). The fact that Thomas footnotes the title of this story in the first edition of *Contes d'Auxois* suggests the group was still unfamiliar to readers when she wrote the story. The FTP would soon, however, count among France's most important resistance groups and would owe its growing reputation to its strategy of coordinating small, anonymous groups, both urban and rural, to sabotage railways and factories serving Nazi interests, to fire on German soldiers, and to punish collaborators. Its increasing effectiveness is borne out by the fact that by fall 1943, Germany deployed troops charged with annihilating the FTP. By 1944, de Gaulle had to reckon with the FTP as a paramilitary force crucial to France's liberation from within; in February of that year, when he called for French resistance groups to unite as the Forces Françaises de l'Intérieur (French Forces of the Interior), the FTP agreed.

René said: "You're not eating here? There's rabbit with potatoes. It's excellent."

He replied: "No, my wife is waiting. She'll let me have it if I'm late."

So René got up and said: "I'll walk part of the way with you. Be right back for my coffee," he called over to the stationmaster.

Then, just as casually, they left, after pausing briefly at the doorway to light their cigarettes.

They walked a short way, then turned onto a little street with grass shooting up between the cobblestones. From time to time, an old woman raises a curtain, then lets it fall. Everybody knows those faces, they are fixtures of the neighborhood. That is René, who works at the train station, and that is Paul, the bank clerk; they have been friends forever. They did their military service together and were both taken prisoner during that "phony war."[2] But they managed to escape before getting sent to Germany. And I know Paul's mother because we went to school together. Paul married a teacher, a little brunette from Paris who thinks somewhat highly of herself, but she's all right. Now

2. Known as the *drôle de guerre*, this period began on 3 September 1939, when France and Britain declared war on Nazi Germany, and ended on 10 May 1940, when Germany invaded Belgium, Luxembourg, Holland, and France. Between these dates, French and British troops waited behind the Maginot Line to face German troops but launched no significant offensives.

René, he's still a boy. It's a shame he hasn't married; he could make some woman very happy. Anyway, that's Paul heading to his home, way down at the end of the street, almost in the fields, a two-story house with a flower garden out front, but he has planted potatoes and spinach in it.

She let the curtain fall again. Nothing ever happens on this street, nothing worth looking at. Not like Grand Square with all the market activity and the Kommandantur that took over the mayor's office; or even rue de la République, now rue du Maréchal-Pétain.

So there's Paul heading home and René walking with him, because they have been friends forever, and that is that.

Paul asked: "Are you positive a train of Germans is coming through tonight at 11:34? You checked it out for yourself?"

"Yes," answered René, "I checked."

"What about the train just before it?" Paul asked.

"It's the freight train that comes through at 10:00. It doesn't stop."

"Five minutes from the train station to the forest," Paul calculates "that means five past ten. It takes a good ten minutes to get from Pierre Levée to the railroad tracks. So, we need to be at Pierre Levée at five minutes before ten. You'll need to go directly to the tracks so you can be sure the freight train has passed by. And you're in charge of letting Louis and Alain know. I'll tell Big Paul." (He is called that because he is a lot taller than Paul or Robert.)

They stopped to light another cigarette.

"I mix my tobacco with corn silk," one of them said because someone was coming. It was the road surveyor, and they greeted him.

"Got it," said René.

"Got it," said Paul.

And Paul pushed open the garden gate; the bell on it rang out in the deserted street. Then there was the sound of his footsteps on the gravel walkway.

So, there's Paul going home for lunch and René going back to the train station: "I'm telling you, Madame Gentillon, we've got to find a wife for that boy."

✶

And now Paul is telling Alice:

"You need to get the word to Big Paul and Robert this afternoon: tonight, five of ten, at Pierre Levée."

She blanched a little, meaning her skin went from pale to more pale. She asks no questions. She waits.

"Tell them not to forget their 'notebooks.'"

She knows what he means by notebooks. But the color has returned to her cheeks. She says nothing. She waits. He adds: "It's for a train."

Then she throws her coat over her shoulders and leaves for the school.

★

She teaches the course for the primary school certificate. And she is quite certain that at least fifteen of her students will have no trouble passing the exam. She makes every effort not to let them see or feel any of her worry. She went to the school library to look for a book. It is *The Song of Roland*. She slipped a note inside. At four o'clock she asked her best student, Marie-Catherine, to stay after class a few minutes. She told her: "Marie-Catherine, take this book and give it to your father; he asked me to get it for him. Don't forget, Marie-Catherine."

But she knows Marie-Catherine never forgets anything.

On her way home, Alice stopped by the shoe shop. The store was crowded. She asked: "When can I bring my wooden shoes in to be repaired? Look, the sole on this one is cracked again."[3]

"That's because they're junk," Big Paul responded.

"Also, I need you to pull a nail out of this one right away, it's hurting my foot."

---

3. Beginning in 1940, France was charged with providing six million pairs of shoes to Germany. French citizens could not purchase new shoes without a provisions card coupon (which was virtually impossible to acquire), and shoe production and repairs for the French were done with wood or paper since all available leather was used for the shoes sent to Germany. Even in peacetime, however, shoes with wooden heels were the norm for poor French schoolchildren in the countryside.

She sat down on a low chair and started to take her shoe off. Meanwhile, the shop cleared out. She said very quickly: "Tonight, five minutes before ten, at Pierre Levée. Don't forget your notebook."

Then she put her shoe back on.

He smiled, and all the lines around his mouth and eyes showed. He was a fit man, about fifty, but he had so many wrinkles. Someone else came into the shop.

"So, when can I bring my wooden shoes in?"

"Not before next week," he replied, "I'm swamped with work."

*

They ate dinner. They listened to the radio. He is pretending to be calm. But she feels his worry. No, not worry, interest, his intense interest in everything. But for her, it is worry. She watches him as she dries the dishes and wonders: "What if this is the last time I ever see him?" She feels her heart beating. She was not meant to be a hero's wife, the kind who hands a shield to her husband or her son and says: "Come back with it, or on it."[4] She was meant for routine, peaceful days: for reading and writing lessons, for dictations, for fixing leaky faucets, for coming home in the evening to clean and cook, for having a child

4. An expression often attributed to Plutarch's *Moralia* (vol. 3, Loeb Classical Library, Harvard UP, 1931), "Come back with your shield, or on it" is what Spartan mothers are supposed to have said to their sons as they saw them off to war (241).

to cradle in her arms, for having a husband to love, and for loving him always.

After all, did she not have everything she needed to make that kind of happiness a reality? But that kind of happiness, she knows, is not possible, and she would have to forget about it, because every moment serves as a reminder that *right now* there can be no happiness, not even the simplest or most humble, without lying or selfishness. Ah, well: happiness would have to be for tomorrow, and for others perhaps. But not for us. And not now.

He has to get going if he does not want to be late. And he cannot be late. But Paul never knows what time it is.

"It's almost a quarter to ten," she says.

He hugged her distractedly. But what if this is the last time, she wonders. She heard his footsteps on the gravel walkway. But not the bell on the gate. She removes it at dusk so no one is alerted to any of their comings and goings at night. By morning, very early, everything is back in place.

*

She grabbed her knitting and her hands move quickly. Then they come to rest on her knees, and all she has left is the waiting, the anxious waiting.

*

There is no moon, but the stars are out. A warm night that already feels like summer. But beneath this beautiful night sky, what are we?

The first thing to do is get out of the city. That is easy: at this hour, no one is out. Besides, if he did run into anyone, he would say it is a beautiful night so he came out to smoke a cigarette before turning in. And besides that, his papers are in order: he is a good, conscientious employee who does his work, and everyone in town knows him. What would be so strange about him stepping out for a cigarette on a beautiful night like this?

He took the little alleyway that runs along the gasworks. The fields are just beyond the hedges, and his feet sink into the soft earth.

Pierre Levée is a crossroads where you will find a tall beech tree but no stone of any kind. Once upon a time a menhir,[5] or something like it, must have stood there; Alice could tell you because she knows all the old stories and all the old names. He thinks about Alice and about how much richer his life has been since they got married. And about how, if she were not his wife, he might not have the courage and the faith to be a man, here, tonight.

---

5. *Pierre Levée* means "raised stone" in French, and *menhir* is formed from the Breton words *maen*, meaning "stone," and *hir*, meaning "long." A menhir is a very large stone that stands alone or in alignment with other stones. Believed to date back as far as six to seven thousand years and distributed throughout Western Europe, menhirs are particularly concentrated in northwestern France and resonate especially with Breton culture, folklore, and history. Single menhirs, often strikingly tall, may have marked important sites or passageways for certain rituals and, later on, routes for religious pilgrimages, or *pardons*, as they are known in Brittany.

A shadow, no, two are visible against the trees at the intersection. He moves in closer: one is Big Paul, the other is Alain. And there is Louis, and here comes Robert.

"René is at the tracks, waiting for us. Have you got the guns? And the lag bolts?"

"Yes, yes," they nod to each other.

But why are these six men here tonight, instead of dozing off drearily to sleep with the rest of this little city?

Big Paul is the one taking the lead. There was a time when he believed in the peaceful transformation of the world, in the disappearance of injustice, in abundance, peace, and joy, when he believed that all you had to do was extend a hand and speak out about justice, and the wealthy would renounce wealth and spread it around. And then, slowly but surely, he learned that nothing is gained without struggle. And that is why he is here now with others who know what they want and who desire the means for obtaining it.

Paul is married to Alice. She taught him that human will makes history and that today, as in the past, this will to be free must be sought out in the history of each day, because history is not something that happens to you, it is something you make happen.

And there is Robert; he is here because he cannot accept that his country has been conquered but does nothing to regain its independence. That is why he has joined those who, no longer waiting for help to come from somewhere else, have decided to fight as long as it takes to liberate his country.

And there is Louis, a tannery worker, here to stand with workers and country folk in the USSR who have achieved liberation and who know what they are defending and dying for.

And there is Alain; not quite seventeen, he is here because he loves to be counted among the fighters—dealing the blows as well as taking them when he has to—and he loves courage, even though he does not know it by name.

And over there, alone in the distance, is René, walking along the railroad tracks, on his way to meet them. René grew up on public assistance. He never knew who his parents were, so he knows how hard this world is for children without parents, and he knows that his job at the train station represents a major achievement for someone like him: "I am proof that anyone can achieve anything they set their minds to in our society." But he knows good and well that this is a lie, because the circumstances you are born into dramatically affect what your future will be. Someday, though, justice will determine everyone's future.

And thus, these six men move silently across the deserted land beneath the naked sky. And because these men are here, in France, as others are across Europe, engaged in an act of will and freedom, something has changed in human history, in this Europe beaten down by stomping boots, this bloodied, faceless, voiceless Europe.

And because these six men are here, with others like them in France and throughout Europe, men who refuse to bow, to be duped, men who are fully committed, something has changed to move people one step away from the abyss and one step closer to the humanity they are not yet but will be tomorrow.

They have reached the main road that cuts through the forest. They stop for a moment and listen intently. Frogs croak. Then the wind blows, stirring the leafless branches. That creaking is the noise of one pine tree trunk rubbing against another.

Amid the sounds of sky and forest, they strain to make out the sounds of humans: footsteps of a patrol guard, an approaching bicycle, an automobile droning in the distance. But there is nothing.

So they hurry across the road, taking cover in the trees on the other side. The railroad tracks are just a couple of yards away. On their way down to the track bed, they see a shadowy figure, someone in a kneeling position, already at work. And now all of them are crouched down or bent over along the tracks, looking like strange gnomes in the bizarre light of their lanterns.

Paul checks his watch: "Are we done?" he asks.

"Yes, we're done," they whisper in response.

They have taken cover in the trees again, submachine guns at their sides.

In the distance they hear the train coming, gathering speed as it leaves the station behind: in just a few more seconds, it will be here.

They see the train's engine roll over on its side, the fuel car right behind it, in a heap of twisted metal. From the other cars that remain on the tracks, they see frightened German soldiers emerge.

Then calmly, the six begin to shoot. Harboring no more hatred than a surgeon would.

Harboring no more hatred.